WHO
KNEW
THERE'D BE
GHOSTS?

WHO KNEW THERE'D BE GHOSTS?

Bill Brittain

drawings by
Michele Chessare

HarperTrophy
A Division of HarperCollins*Publishers*

Designed by Joyce Hopkins

Library of Congress Cataloging-in-Publication Data
Brittain, Bill.
    Who knew there'd be ghosts?

    Summary: Three spunky youngsters join forces with two
lively ghosts to save a historic mansion from being
destroyed by a crooked antique dealer.
    1. Children's stories, American.   [1. Ghosts—Fiction]
I. Chessare, Michele, ill.   II. Title.
PZ7.B78067Wh   1985   [Fic]   84-48496
ISBN 0-06-020699-3
ISBN 0-06-020700-0 (lib. bdg.)
ISBN 0-06-440224-X (pbk.)

First Harper Trophy edition, 1988.

For "The Buffalo Bunch"—
who have my undying gratitude

Contents

Fancy Shoes
and Black Boots

At first, nobody really believed in the ghosts. Least of all Harry or Books or me.

But by the time last summer was over, almost everybody in Bramton had seen Horace and Essie—heard 'em talking and everything. Sure, those two sly Parnells would fade away and pop into view again like a TV picture on a stormy night; but enough of 'em showed so they could be recognized for what they were.

Since then, ghost hunters and so-called occult scientists have been coming around to visit the old house on Spring Street. If one or both of the Parnells feel like making an appearance, they'll put a real scare into whoever comes calling. Then a story about the Parnells will come out in a magazine or newspaper. But the story'll always talk about "collective hysteria" or "mass delusion," as if Horace and Essie weren't real and anybody who thinks different is soft in the head.

Oh, they're real, all right. The people of Bramton are kind of proud that Horace and Essie live in our village—although I guess the word "live" doesn't apply to ghosts. But where those two Parnells would be today if Harry the Blimp and Books and I hadn't overheard Fancy Shoes and Black Boots talking . . . well, that's anybody's guess.

It all started that first week in August, with Harry, Books, and me playing one of our games at the Parnell place. The three of us have been best friends since second grade. That was five years ago, and five years is a long time to have the same best friends. The truth is, most of the other kids don't have a lot to do with us. They say we're weird.

We're not, though. Different, maybe. But not weird.

Take Harry the Blimp, for example. Harry Troy's his real name, but everybody calls him Harry the Blimp because of his size. He's almost six feet tall and must weigh close to two hundred pounds. He's got a big moon face and looks like he's hiding an inflated inner tube under his shirt. Harry will never get an A+ in the brains department, but he's really a good-natured guy, and I've never seen him get angry at anybody, no matter how much they laugh at him on account of his size. Maybe that's why Harry likes hanging around with Books and me. We don't laugh at him.

Books Scofield's the only girl I know who can't make up her mind whether she wants to be a college professor or the bantamweight boxing champion of the world. She usually wears old blue jeans and dirty white sneakers and tee shirts with things like SAVE THE WHALES on 'em. She's got freckles and short brown hair and a left hook that could knock the head off a gorilla. Her real name's Wendy, but everybody calls her Books because there doesn't seem to be anything she doesn't know. She doesn't study more than anybody else, but whenever test marks come out, there's Wendy Scofield's name at the top of the list. Books doesn't make a big thing of being the class brain, even though it bugs a lot of her classmates. She's a good friend, and I don't think she's weird at all.

Me? My name's Tommy Donahue. And I have a way of doing everything wrong. You know what I mean. Give me an arithmetic problem where two numbers just beg to be multiplied, and I'll start doing long division, quicker'n scat. On dress-up day at school, when all the boys wear jackets and ties and look their best, I'll forget and put on my shirt with a torn pocket and pants with a hole in the knee. Put me in a basketball game, and the first time I get the ball I'll stuff it in the wrong basket so the other team gets two points. Dad once said that if everybody in the world was starving and it started raining chicken soup, I'd be the only one who'd run outside holding a fork.

But the one thing I *have* got is a good imagination. I dream up most of the games that Harry the Blimp and Books and I enjoy so much. Things like King Arthur and his knights invade the Land of the Hobbits, or Robin Hood and his Merry Men climb Mount Olympus. Sometimes we have a little trouble with Books, who won't sit still for being Maid Marian or Queen Guinevere while Harry the Blimp and I have all the fun. Usually she figures out some way to put Marian or Guinevere asleep for a thousand years or have them held for ransom in a far-off land. Then she becomes an Amazon warrior or the bandit Belle Starr, and she's happy again.

For our games, you can't go to a park or playground. I mean, it's embarrassing to be at the Sheriff of Nottingham's archery contest, flexing an imaginary bow and getting set to shoot at a target a hundred paces away when somebody's screaming in your ear to get off the handball court and all the grown-ups are laughing their heads off at you.

That's why we liked playing at Parnell House so much. Three whole acres, right in the middle of town, with no people around to bother us. The younger kids were scared of the place, and the older ones didn't want to get their clothes dirty. But we three thought the place was swell. There were old, twisted trees to climb, and high grass to hide in, and a swampy spot where you could catch frogs. There was even a graveyard out in back with a big stone monument in the center. The monument was two pieces of granite that must have had a high polish before the weather got to them. One piece lay across the top of the other like the letter *T*, with sockets gouged out at each end of the *T*'s crosspiece. All the gravestones around the monument had Parnell carved on 'em, with odd first names like Jethro and Martita.

A rusty iron fence surrounded the property, making it easy to imagine we were playing in the courtyard of a castle. The castle, of course, was Parnell House itself. Set high on a hill, it overlooked the whole village. It was all gray and dingy, with clapboards hanging loose and knocking about in the wind, and shingles falling off the roof from time to time. The glass in all the windows had been smashed long ago, and the openings were boarded up. One of the two chimneys at the ends of the house had collapsed, and it looked like the other one might fall down at any time.

Still, the place had a kind of dignity about it, like a fine lady who'd fallen on hard times. In its day it must have been real fancy. There were a lot of people in Bramton who wanted to see it fixed up and turned into a museum. They'd collected a little money for the purpose, but not nearly enough. And if repairs weren't started soon, it wouldn't be long before the house would fall down all by itself.

Now you're not to tell Mom and Dad this next part,

because they gave me strict orders not to go inside that house. But one day Harry the Blimp put his shoulder to the rear door, and with a lot of pushing and creaking of rusty hinges, he managed to get it open.

Inside, it was hot and stuffy, and the stink of rotten wood was enough to make you choke. But we sneaked around through the two big rooms on the main floor with only the light from the open door to see by. There was no furniture. Just some hunks of wood lying on the floor. But each room had a fireplace big enough to walk into, and both fireplaces had mantels that were big slabs of solid oak. Words were carved in each slab, and Books lit matches so we could read 'em.

The one where the chimney had collapsed said:

THO' YOU REST AFAR, YOU ARE IN OUR HEARTS

And the other:

PARNELL—1748

We didn't stay in there very long that day. Not even long enough to go upstairs or down cellar. The excuse we made to one another was that the steps looked too weak to hold us. And anyway, there wasn't enough light to see by.

But those weren't the real reasons. Y'see, all the time we were in that house, I couldn't get over the

feeling that somebody—or some *thing*—was watching us. A couple of times, I just knew eyes were staring at my back, but though I turned around real fast, I never saw anything. Later, Harry and Books told me they'd felt the same thing.

It was our second time inside when we saw the stain on the floor. A narrow line of dampness that made a perfect circle about three feet across, right at the bottom of the stairs. Books leaned down, rubbed at the stain, and then sniffed her fingers.

"Seems to be water," she said.

"Prob'ly the roof leaks" was Harry's guess.

Books shook her head. "Leaks make spots, not circles. And there hasn't been any rain in two weeks."

"Maybe somebody came in here earlier and made the circle just for a joke," Harry replied.

But he didn't believe that for a minute, any more than Books or I did. We all knew about the rumors that even though the house had been abandoned for years, Parnells still inhabited it.

Oh, not living people.

Ghosts.

Lots of Bramton people had stories of hearing strange and eerie sounds after dark when they walked by Parnell House. Mayor Alonzo Peace once reported a hideous groaning from the cellar as he strolled home after a Village Council meeting. But when he sent the police to investigate, they found nothing.

Ghosts.

Right then and there, we decided we'd be better off playing outside.

All of which brings me up to that first week in August, with the three of us lying on our bellies beneath that spruce tree and hearing . . . Well, let me start at the beginning.

The day had started off as a real bummer. I was sitting in our living room, trying to get two parts of a model plane to fit together. Dad—he's a lawyer, and he handles all the village's business—was in the little room he calls an office, making a phone call. I wasn't paying much attention until I heard Dad say something that made me sit up and really listen hard.

"Well, now that you've seen Parnell House, what do you think of it? That place could be a real buy for the right person."

Parnell House—was somebody going to buy Parnell House?

"I don't think Mayor Peace and the Village Council would accept an offer that low," Dad went on. "Oh, I know the house is in bad shape. But it's on prime land, right in the middle of town."

That was our playground he was talking about! He was getting ready to sell it.

"Of course. I can take you out there for another look around any time you say. I'm sure we can come to some agreement. If we could strike a deal, the council could approve it right away. There's a meeting next Friday."

That's when I dashed outside and headed for Parnell House on the run. No more playground! I had to tell Books and Harry the bad news.

An hour later, Books and Harry and I were sitting on a big rock in the Parnell side yard, staring glumly at one another. I guess my news ruined their day, too.

"Good-bye playground," said Harry sadly.

"Well, I'm not about to start playing in any dumb old park," said Books with an angry shake of her head. "We've got to do something about this."

"But what?" I asked.

We thought about that question all morning and got absolutely nowhere.

After lunch, we started playing a game I'd dreamed up, just to get our minds off our troubles.

Daniel Boone was on the trail of marauding Indians who were getting ready to attack the settlement. Naturally I was Daniel, and Harry the Blimp was my faithful companion, Jethro. Books got to be all the Indians.

We kept on with the game all afternoon. Sometimes we had to let the Indians win, just so Books would keep on playing.

Just before suppertime, Daniel and Jethro were traveling one last trail. We weren't having much luck at finding Indians though, because Books had picked herself a real good hiding place.

Finally Harry and I sat down on the ground to rest. I couldn't help wondering what would happen to our playground when the house was sold. And if some—some *thing*—did inhabit Parnell House, what would happen to *it*?

That's when I heard the owl hooting around in front of the house. But owls don't hoot in the daytime. It was Books, giving our special signal. It meant: *Strangers are coming. Hide yourselves, quick!*

Harry the Blimp and I crawled under a big spruce tree in the backyard and lay flat on our bellies. The lower limbs of the tree bent almost to the ground, covering us like a giant umbrella. Nobody'd see us unless they leaned way down. Books must have spotted that hiding place, too, because a few seconds later she wriggled in to join us.

"A big car pulled up in front," Books whispered into my left ear as I lay there sandwiched between her and Harry. "I gave the signal and then legged it back here. Listen."

Footsteps. And it sounded like they were coming right toward us. As they got closer, we could hear two men mumbling to one another.

Finally the footsteps stopped, just as I thought whoever it was would walk right into us. I lifted my head and peered out from beneath the tree.

Just beyond where the branches bent to the ground stood two men. From under the tree, all we could see were their feet. The man on the right wore what looked almost like slippers of polished brown leather, with fancy stitching and little tassels on the top. The other one had on heavy, worn black boots laced with leather thongs.

"Well, there's the house. I wanted you to see it up close in daylight before you started your search. That thing's got to be in there somewhere. D'you think you'll be able to find it?"

I guessed it was Fancy Shoes doing the talking. He had a habit of tapping his foot along with the words.

"No problem," answered Black Boots. "But if I can only search at night and have to be careful not to make too much noise, it'll take time."

"How much time?"

"Hard to say. It could be hidden anywhere. Behind the walls, maybe, or under a floor. Could be I'll have to wreck the whole house to find it. Maybe a week—maybe more."

"Can you start right away—tonight?" Fancy Shoes asked.

"I don't know. First I've got to find out when the police car goes by here . . . who takes walks late in the evening . . . that kind of thing. That could take a few hours or a few days. I don't want somebody busting in on me while I'm looking around. What's the hurry, anyway?"

"I've offered to buy the house from the village. A lawyer named Donahue is handling the deal, and he's getting anxious for me to name a price the council will accept."

Beneath the tree, I rolled my eyes first at Books and then at Harry. They both looked as scared as I felt. Fancy Shoes was talking about my father.

"But I don't want the house," Fancy Shoes went on. "Just what's inside it. Oh, I'll buy the place if I have to. But everything would be a lot easier if you found that thing before the Village Council meeting next Friday. Then we could take it away with nobody being the wiser."

Black Boots crunched through the dry weeds to the back door. "Somebody's been around here," he said. "The door's been forced open."

"Take it easy. It was probably just those fool kids who play here sometimes. But they always leave before dark. Everybody's scared to come here at night. They think the place is haunted. So even if you do make some noise while you're looking around, people will just think it's the ghosts, having a good time."

"I hope you're right," said Black Boots. "If anybody catches me inside, I'm gonna have to play rough."

"Now, now," cautioned Fancy Shoes. "No need for

that. Nobody knows what's in there. Except us, that is. I'm supposed to be an honest businessman. If somebody got hurt, it could ruin me."

"You worry too much," said Black Boots. "Look, maybe I'll get lucky and find it right away."

"Maybe. But if you have to rip the whole place apart, go ahead. Just find it."

Fancy Shoes and Black Boots stood staring at the house for what seemed like a couple of centuries. But finally we heard footsteps walking away. We stayed under the tree for another ten minutes or so, just to make sure the coast was clear. Then Books sneaked out the far side, scurried behind a row of dead grapevines, and peeked at the road. She returned with good news.

"They've gone. You can come out."

Harry the Blimp and I crawled into the open and stood up. "What were those two guys talking about?" Harry asked. "I heard 'em, but I didn't understand 'em."

Books sat on the ground, and for a long time she seemed to be talking to herself. Finally she looked up at Harry and me.

"I understood a lot," she said. "The man with the tasseled shoes wants Parnell House. But he doesn't really want it. See?"

Both Harry and I shook our heads.

"He wants something that's *in* the house," Books went on. "And Black Boots is going to come looking for it during the nights. Meanwhile, Fancy Shoes will pretend to be dickering with Tommy's father."

"If they don't really want the house," said Harry with a smile, "then our playground is safe."

"Safe?" said Books. "Nothing's safe as long as Black Boots is around. Didn't you hear what he said about playing rough?"

"I bet I'm stronger than he is," said Harry proudly.

"Don't talk like a jerk, Harry!" said Books. "Black Boots is even bigger'n you. And I'll bet he carries a gun or a knife or something besides. You tangle with him, and you could get hurt—bad."

"But what do you suppose they're looking for, Books?" I asked. "Diamonds? Gold?"

"Not likely, Tommy. You've been reading too many adventure stories. The Parnells wouldn't have gone away leaving stuff like that around."

"Then what—"

"I don't know," said Books. "What I know is we've got to do something. Otherwise, either Black Boots is going to tear down Parnell House to find what he's looking for, or else Fancy Shoes will buy the place. Either way, we lose our playground."

If we had to start playing in the park, it'd be . . . *yucck!* I tried to think of something. But even Daniel Boone and Jethro couldn't take on somebody like Black Boots. "What can we do, Books?" I asked finally. "Tell our parents?"

"Ah, they wouldn't believe us," said Harry. "My folks never listen to anything I say. They'd just start asking why we were hanging around here in the first place."

"Harry's right," said Books. "It's our playground, so we've got to handle this ourselves."

"But how?" I asked.

"Black Boots is going to come back here soon—maybe tonight. So we've got to stand guard on Parnell House. All night, every night, until we find out what's going on."

"Right," said Harry. "And if Black Boots comes along, we'll jump out and grab him and—"

"No—we—will—not!" said Books sternly. "When he comes, we sneak away and tell the police that some-body's in Parnell House. Let them handle Black Boots. That way, nobody gets hurt. Okay?"

I had to think about this. Sitting inside that spooky old house all night with Black Boots ready to pop in at any moment wasn't really my idea of a roaring good time. But it seemed like the only answer. "I guess I can get out," I said finally. "I'll meet you and Harry right here at—"

"Hold it, Tommy," said Books. "Wrong."

"What do you mean?"

"If all three of us start sneaking off every night, there's a good chance at least one of our parents will find out something's going on."

"Then what—"

"We'll take turns. I'll take tomorrow night because we're going to my aunt's house this evening, and we won't be home until real late."

"Dad's painting my room," said Harry the Blimp. "And I'm sleeping with my brother. I'd never get out without waking him up. But I'll be glad to take the night after you, Books."

With that, both Books and Harry the Blimp looked straight at me.

"Hey, wait a minute!" I cried. "I don't want to be the first to—"

"The castle and the courtyard," said Books.

"And the games," added Harry the Blimp.

Five minutes later I was trudging toward home, committed to spending the night in Parnell House, waiting to see if Black Boots would return.

Getting out of my house that night wasn't much of a trick. Before bedtime, I put a big candle and some matches in a dresser drawer. When I went to bed, I just took off my shoes, lying under the sheet with all my clothes on.

The clock in the tower of the village hall had just bonged twelve when Dad began his snoring. Believe me, when that sound starts, you could drive a herd of elephants right through the upstairs hall and nobody'd notice. I got up, put on my shoes, and stuffed the candle and matches into a pocket. Then down the stairs, past the door of Dad's office, and out the front way.

Ten minutes later I was standing in front of Parnell House. There was a big full moon in the sky, giving me dim light to see by and at the same time creating enough shadows to hide an army of ghouls and demons.

As I walked around to the rear, briars clawed at my pant legs like hands reaching up out of the ground. At the back door I stopped long enough to light the candle. Then I inched my way inside.

The smell of rot was thick in the air, and as I walked to the stairs, the floorboards creaked and sagged with each step. The stairs screeched and howled like a damned soul when I climbed them. Somebody just had to hear me in there.

But when I got to the second floor and stopped to catch my breath, the whole house was as quiet as death.

By the light of the candle, I saw four doorways off the upstairs hallway. I picked the first one on the right simply because the door was already open. I thought that if I heard Black Boots downstairs I could leap out and— And what? My plans hadn't gotten that far.

The room I'd picked was in almost as bad shape as

the big ones downstairs. The plaster had fallen off the walls in a couple of places, and the floorboards were rotten. In the middle of the room was a three-legged table with a little bench beside it. A wide, deep closet took up one corner. The sides of the closet weren't quite the same dingy color as the room's walls, and I guessed it had been added some time after the house itself was built. Its door was closed, and nothing in the world would have made me open it.

The flickering candle provided plenty of shadowy corners. I thought that there was enough light to see anything coming to get me—just before it ripped my heart out with its fangs.

Great . . . terrific. In there only five minutes, and already I was scaring myself silly. There are no such things as demons, I told myself firmly. Vampires and ghosts and such things exist only in your imagina—

"Aaarrrrgghhh!"

Sweat popped out on my forehead, and my heart did a loop-the-loop in my chest. The moan had an unearthly quality, like shouting down a well. Games or no games, I'd gladly have left the house that minute—except that the sound had come from the hallway just outside.

A million years later, the village clock bonged one. I'd just about convinced myself that the ghastly moan had come from a cat sitting on a fence somewhere, when—

"Ohh! Ooohhhhhh!"

The sound was softer this time. Exactly like a woman crying. And again it came from the hall outside the room.

I thought about blowing out the candle. But that would leave me in the dark. No way. Ghosts do not exist, I told myself again. It was just my imagination and that spooky room, getting together to drive me up the wall with fright.

I set the candle on the table in a little pool of wax and tiptoed to the boarded-up window. Through a tiny crack between two of the boards I could see almost the whole village of Bramton in the moonlight. As I looked, the traffic light downtown turned from green to red, and a big pizza sign blinked on and off.

That glimpse of the real world made me feel better. "Tommy Donahue, you're a real fool," I said in a whisper. "Now you forget about those crazy sounds. Probably just the wind. March right back to that bench and keep guard." Both Dad and Mom would have been proud of that little lecture I gave myself.

I turned around.

That's when my blood turned to ice cubes, and I started trembling as if something invisible was shaking me by the shoulders. There it sat on the table—a thing that hadn't been there before.

It was a human head.

I couldn't speak or even move. All I could do was

stare at that—that thing on the table. It was the head of a man. A man who'd spent a lot of time outdoors, for the skin was tanned and leathery. The hair was in a kind of braid in back, and wiry whiskers covered the chin and upper lip. The eyes were closed.

And then the eyes popped open. They looked straight at me. At the same time, a horrible scowl twisted the whiskery face. The head spoke to me in a hollow, ghostly voice:

"Get out of my house at once!"

Horace and Essie

The head kept looking at me, twisting itself into one hideous expression after another. I stared at it, frozen with fear.

The lips puckered. *"Boo!"* cried the head in a loud voice.

I jumped back and banged against the wall. My mouth opened wide and I tried to yell, but all that came out was a hoarse gurgle.

"Begone from Parnell House this instant, young mortal!" ordered the head with a hollow moan.

"Yes, sir," I croaked. "I—I didn't mean any harm." I began inching toward the door, keeping as far away from the head as possible. "I was just kind of standing guard."

At that, the head's fearsome scowl disappeared. In its place came a look of—of confusion and curiosity.

I'd almost reached the door and was about to run for the stairs when the head spoke again.

"Come back here, lad."

I wanted to run away. But if I did, who knew what the head would do? "Wha—what do you want?" I asked.

"Your name, boy—what is it?"

"Thomas. Thomas Donahue."

"And you say you were standing guard, eh? Guard against what, young Thomas?"

"Two men. They were here this afternoon. And they—"

"Aye. Heard 'em myself, I did, from my resting place in the cellar."

"Resting place?" I asked. "You mean you get tired, just like—like humans?"

"A bit like that. 'Tis the sun that does it. Drains my strength like water leaking from a cracked bucket, though I can still hear well enough. But night is the only time when a ghost can be up and about."

"A ghost!" I cried, and a shiver prickled its way along my spine.

"Of course. What else would I be? But those men you spoke of—they seemed to be looking for something?"

"Yes, sir. And they said they'd tear down this house to get it, if they had to."

"And you'd save the house if you can, young Thomas. Is that it?"

I nodded, feeling cold sweat run down my face. "My friends and I—we play outside. And we don't want to lose our playground. I mean—"

"I've heard ye, while lying helpless in the cellar during daylight hours. Two lads and a girl." And then the horrible frown appeared again. "Are you sure you've not come to Parnell House for some deviltry, boy?"

My throat was so tight from fear I couldn't speak anymore. I just shook my head.

"Then 'tis a fool I am!" roared the head with a hearty laugh. "Trying to drive you off with groans and shrieks and such."

"So it was you who—"

"Aye, lad. Mortals fear ghosts worse'n the plague and wish only to be rid of them. Likewise we ghosts have a dread of most humans and will do anything to drive 'em away from our domain."

"I—I see. Then maybe I'd better just go . . ."

"Nay, young Thomas. Stay. You're a brave young'un, and I respect that. Though palsied with fright, you didn't leave your post here. Remarkable."

"If you don't mind, sir, I'd rather go away and—"

"You've naught to fear from me, young Thomas. Truth to tell, we have a mutual problem, and I could use your help on it. So please, consider yourself my guest. And stop that confounded cowering and quaking. How can we be friends when you're scared to look upon me?"

"But is—is there any more of you? I mean—"

"Ah, that's what's got the wind up, is it? Very well, then."

The room was suddenly filled with the stench of sweat and gunpowder. At the same time, something began to appear next to the table. At first I could look right through it at the discolored wall beyond.

Slowly the body came into view. It wore pants of wool stuffed into worn knee boots. The shirt of homespun cloth had full sleeves and was laced at the neck. Over the shirt the body wore a kind of long vest of greasy leather, with rude stitching holding the seams together. Through the vest's opening I saw an ancient flintlock pistol tucked into a wide belt.

But it was the shirt's collar that horrified me. Dark, reddish-brown stains covered it, and—and—

There was nothing above the collar. The body had no head.

It stretched out its arms. Groping fingers found the head, lifted it, and placed it on the body's shoulders. When the head was properly fitted into place, the man looked straight at me.

"Is my appearance more to your liking now, young Thomas?"

"Yes, sir. But who are you?"

"The devil take me, sir! I'm a noddy, and I crave your pardon. My attempts to scare you off must have addled my wits. Horace Parnell, at your service."

He bowed low, and I was afraid the head might fall off again. Then he put out a hand for me to shake.

But when I tried, my fingers curled around—nothing!

"I forgot myself," said Horace. "A ghost, such as myself, cannot touch that which is mortal."

"But Mr.—Horace?"

"Yes, young Thomas?"

"How did you get to *be* a ghost?"

"The story's a long one. But we've the rest of the night to while away. 'Twas my father, Abram Parnell, who built this house in 1748 as a home for his new bride, Abigail. This land was frontier then, and the house was the wonder of the area, where most folk lived in log cabins. Bram, as my father was called, was a merchant, selling tools, milling the grain of the farmers, and finding markets for their crops. He was hugely successful, and the house was raised as a symbol of his success.

"Soon a village grew here. Bram's Town it was called, and later changed to Bramton. I was to take over the business from my father one day. But that was not to be."

"Oh? Why not?"

"I was a headstrong lad, and when the colonies

began their fight to be free of British rule, naught would do but for me to enlist in the colonial army. Easy duty it was, at first. Spring and summer of 1776 saw me in Philadelphia town, hunting quail and catching trout to grace the tables of the members of the Continental Congress meeting there. Those gentlemen even presented me with a letter of commendation for my fine work in providing their tastier victuals.

"But scarce a year later, I was with the army of General Horatio Gates, up around Albany in New York Colony. We were to stop the British general, Johnny Burgoyne, from bringing his army down from the north and splitting the colonies like a ripe melon.

"Near Albany both armies dug in, neither one able to gain the advantage. Gates had need of somebody who'd carry messages to Burgoyne and back so the rules of battle could be agreed upon. I was the man chosen for the job."

"But wouldn't the British soldiers shoot you?"

Horace shook his head. "I carried a white flag so the lobsterbacks would know I bore messages," he said. "But one day, walking toward the British lines, I got a stone in my boot. To rid myself of it, I put down the white flag to pull off my boot. There I was, hopping about on one foot, when I heard someone running behind me. I turned just in time to see a redcoat coming at me, his sword flashing in the sun. A terrible pain shot across my neck, and my head hit the ground with a wallop. The last I remember as my eyes dimmed in death was seeing my own body at the far side of the path. That fool lobsterback had taken my head off with a single swipe of his sword."

"That's awful, Horace," I said. "But I still don't understand why you're a— I mean—"

"A ghost?" replied Horace. "The way of it is this, young Thomas. My father, Abram Parnell, made a solemn wish on his deathbed. It was his desire that every Parnell of the family he'd founded would come back here to die and be buried in the family cemetery. And a dying wish is a powerful thing indeed. Most of the family held to that wish. But after my untimely death, all that was sent back here were my journals— diaries, you'd call them—of my life as a soldier, and a tin lockbox with my personal papers. My body— and my head—rest in an unmarked grave near Albany. And since my body couldn't find its rest in the family burial plot, my spirit is condemned to abide in this house forever, never to go beyond its walls, no matter what."

"But doesn't it get awfully lonely?" I asked.

From somewhere in the room came a girlish giggle. "Not a bit of it," said a lilting voice. "Horace has me for company."

A big ring of water began dripping from—from somewhere onto the floor of the room. Then, slowly, the girl appeared, standing in the center of the ring.

She was perhaps a couple of years older than I was, and she wore an old-fashioned dress of silk and lace. From her waist, a wide hoopskirt belled out, reaching the floor. She would have been pretty, except—

From head to toe she was drenched with water. Her dark hair hung limply down her back, and drops glistened on her bare shoulders. What I'd first taken for a necklace was the stem of a water lily coiled about her neck. Her dress was completely soaked, and the ring on the floor was from water that was constantly dripping from the hem of her skirt.

The circle of water—the one Books and Harry and I had seen the first time we'd entered Parnell House. She must have been standing right on that spot!

"Young Thomas," said Horace, "may I present Miss Esmeralda Parnell—Essie, to her friends."

"Thomas—what a charmin' name," she said. "An' so handsome a lad, too. Not a bit frightening, the way most mortals are. I know I'm just gonna love chattin' with you."

"How do you do, ma'am," I whispered.

"Oh, poo! Don't be so solemn and proper. Call me Essie."

"Yes, ma'am—I mean, Essie."

"There, that's better. I declare, Thomas, you've been talking far too long with Horace, and you've taken on some of his more unpleasant aspects. That man knows simply nothing about the social graces."

"My time upon this earth was one of hardship and fighting for the cause of freedom," Horace snapped. "We had little time for the social niceties and empty compliments that so delight you, Esmeralda."

"There you go—growling again," Essie told Horace. "But after more than a century of your righteous prating, I now have more pleasant company, thank you."

With a proud shake of her head, Essie turned to me. "Like Horace, I was denied burial in the family plot. My story's ever so tragic. Would you like to hear it, Thomas?"

"Y—yes, Essie," I said with a gulp. "Please."

" 'Twas the summer of fifty-seven," she began. "That's *eighteen* fifty-seven, Thomas. By then, the family wealth had increased almost beyond reckoning. Daddy had to travel south for some business dealings. Mama and I were to come along, too. Imagine li'l ol' me, riding that big steamboat all the way down the Mississippi to New Orleans."

The way Essie said it, it sounded like "N'Awlins."

"One evening I walked out on the main deck alone. The stars were bright, and the big paddlewheel at the stern of the *Belle of Natchez* was moving us along at a fine rate. It was ever so romantic. I was rather hoping one of the handsome young men aboard would come by and strike up a conversation. I thought how beautiful I'd look with my back arched, staring up at the slipper of a moon. So I leaned back against the rail. Only—only—"

"Go ahead, Essie," chuckled Horace. "Tell him."

"Only when I leaned back, there wasn't any rail," Essie snapped with an angry stomp of her foot. "Some half-witted dock worker had taken down that section of railing earlier in the day to bring cargo aboard, and he'd failed to replace it. Down I went, straight into the water, with none of the other passengers any the wiser. The boat steamed off without me. I didn't know how to swim—no *real* lady did then—and all those skirts and petticoats and pantaloons I wore soaked up water and dragged me down.

"I drowned, Thomas. Alas, I was so beautiful."

Horace snorted loudly and covered a wide grin with the back of his hand. Essie scowled darkly at him before going on.

"My body was never found. My bones are deep in the mud of the Mississippi. Father and Mother were grief-stricken, of course. Of all my belongings, Mother kept only a small ring with an emerald stone to remember me by. Father built the monument in the graveyard for me, and had the fireplace mantel replaced and a new inscription carved. A team of workmen were here nearly a week completing those tasks. I could hear them from my resting place in the cellar—though of course during the sunlight hours I couldn't watch."

"But during the dark hours you'd sneak up to see what had been done," said Horace with a chuckle. "Ah, Thomas, the foolish pride Essie exhibited the night after that mantel was laid in place would have shamed a peacock."

"Of course I was proud," said Essie, pouting prettily. "Those words on the mantel—'Tho' you rest afar, you are in our hearts'—aren't they lovely, Thomas? Oh, if only I'd dared appear to Papa and Mama. But the fright they'd have gotten on seeing me as a ghost would have been the death of them."

Essie sighed deeply and spread her hands wide. "So here I am—condemned to inhabit Parnell House throughout eternity."

"Essie's was the last generation of wealthy Parnells," said Horace. "During the Civil War the southern markets dried up, and the business failed. When the last of the family money was spent, this house had to be rented for whatever use could be made of it. For a time it was a general store. Later, it became a tavern, frequented by sots and drunkards of the lowest sort. After that, a rooming house for the dregs of humanity, run by a woman known as Whiskey Maude, who rented straw mattresses for a penny a night. Finally the house was abandoned, to fall into decay, as you see it now."

"But Parnells still returned to be buried in family earth," added Essie. "The last was Jesse Parnell, back in 1939. And now Horace and I abide in Parnell House alone. Every night we watch at the windows, seeing the passing of the seasons and the changes that have taken place across the years in Bramton village. But if any of those—those *people*—come too close, we moan and cry, hoping to frighten them off. If mortals find us horrible to look upon, we find them just as frightening."

Essie looked at me and simpered. "Course that doesn't apply to *you*, Thomas. You're very sweet."

I felt my face getting red. "Must you embarrass the lad?" Horace demanded.

"Oh, la! There you go, complaining again, Horace Parnell. As the centuries go by, you remain as cold and stern as ever."

"The changes we've watched through chinks in the boarded windows addle the mind and numb the brain," Horace told me. "Lanterns lighting up the streets, yet there's no flame inside, but just an orb of glowing glass. Iron birds flying through the air. Coaches traveling the roads with no horses to be seen. One day you must tell me where they hide the animals, Thomas."

"And women, cutting their hair short and wearing trousers just like men," snorted Essie. "Disgusting!"

"Enough about us," said Horace. "Young Thomas, tell us more of the two men who would tear down Parnell House."

It didn't take long to tell what I knew of the plans of Fancy Shoes and Black Boots.

"Hmm," mused Horace when I'd finished. "I'd not have thought anything in Parnell House had value enough to interest anyone."

"If those two want something in here," said Essie, "they'll bring this place down around our ears. And what then, Horace? What becomes of us when our home is no more?"

" 'Tis a fearsome plight indeed," said Horace. And then he stared at me, long and hard. "But mayhap all is not lost," he went on. "Perhaps we have a common cause here, young Thomas. You and your friends, and Essie and me. That makes five. Five against two—rather good odds, that. Let us resolve now to prevent those men of whom you spoke from carrying out their evil plans."

"But Horace," said Essie, "we are but ghosts! We're confined to this house as if locked in prison. And even at that, we may appear only during the hours between sunset and sunrise. While Thomas and his friends are so—so—"

"Young?" said Horace. "Joan of Arc was in her teens when she led the armies of France. When but a youth, Alexander the Great conquered all the known world of his time. And Thomas and his friends are no less than they. Take courage, young Thomas. We'll overcome the blaggards yet!"

Courage? Me? Boy, were they talking to the wrong person. Still, if we were going to keep the playground, I had to do *something*. Besides, saying no to a couple of ghosts didn't seem very wise.

"I'll try," I said weakly.

As I spoke, the village clock struck five. I went to the window and looked through the crack between the boards. I could see the outline of the trees outside, and the slate gray of the sky.

"The night is over," said Essie. As I turned around, she and Horace began to fade away.

"Wait!" I called to them. "What am I supposed to—"

But I was shouting in an empty room.

I took a deep breath. The stink of sweat and gunpowder was still in the air. And by the dim light of the candle I could see a dark ring of water on the floor.

Black Boots wouldn't be coming with dawn breaking. I creaked my way out of the old house and ran all the way back home. Once in my own room, I peeled off my clothes and got into bed. But I wondered if I'd ever fall asleep.

That was the last thing I remembered until nine-thirty.

I'd only gotten about four hours' sleep, and I got out of bed feeling like I'd been dragged through a knothole. Even after I'd washed and dressed, I still wasn't fully awake. I slogged down the stairs, heading for the kitchen and breakfast.

But as I passed the door of Dad's office, I saw something that jolted me fully awake.

Dad had a client in there with him. I couldn't see who it was because the visitor's chair was way in the corner where it was hidden from my view.

But I did get a good look at the client's feet.

He wore shoes that looked almost like slippers of polished brown leather, with fancy stitching and little tassels on the top.

Return to
Parnell House

Now you might think that as soon as I spotted Fancy Shoes, I'd go rushing into the office to warn Dad about what was going on and ask him for help in saving Parnell House. But that's because you don't know what Dad's like.

Oh, he's okay—I mean, he *is* my father, after all. But he's always so darn practical, and he's got about as much imagination as a bowl of cold oatmeal. He thinks the adventure books I read are a waste of time, and as for the games us kids play at Parnell House, every time I talk about them he looks like he's sucking a prune. According to him, I should only read things that will improve my mind *(ugh!)* and play games like baseball with the guys on the next block (double *ugh!*).

Once in a magazine I found a picture of an ink-blot, and you were supposed to say what it looked like, and that way you could tell what kind of person you were. I saw two knights battling with swords, and Mom said it was a beautiful butterfly. But Dad? He looked at the blot for about five minutes and then told us both to stop being silly, it was just a spot of ink. Imagination? None.

When I was real small, I'd sometimes lie in bed at night and hear sounds coming from downstairs. So I'd run to my parents' room and tell Dad there were burglars in the house. But he'd just mutter something about the house settling and how foolish I was acting. Then he'd roll over and go back to sleep. Okay, the next morning we'd go downstairs and nothing would have been touched, and Dad would say that proved he was right and I'd just let my imagination run away with me again. But I'd have slept better if he'd at least gone and looked.

Tell him about Fancy Shoes and Black Boots and a couple of ghosts I'd met last night? Not likely.

"Frankly, the Village Council hoped to get a bit more for the Parnell place than what you're offering," Dad was saying to Fancy Shoes. "And there are some others interested in the place. They'd like to make a local museum out of it."

"I've done a little checking," replied Fancy Shoes in that same smooth voice I'd heard yesterday, "and those museum people don't have enough money to even begin repairs on that old house. I think my offer of forty is rather generous. Perhaps a bit too generous.

It's possible I could change my mind and withdraw it at any time."

Especially if you and Black Boots find what you're looking for, I thought.

"Let's not be hasty," Dad said. "Naturally I can neither accept your offer nor turn it down right now. That's up to the Village Council when they meet on Friday."

"Right now I believe that with some fixing up, Parnell House would make me a nice home," said Fancy Shoes. "You'd better hope I feel the same way on Friday."

That's when both Dad and Fancy Shoes got up from their chairs and started walking out of the office.

If they found me lurking outside the office door, Dad would have six kinds of fits. He's told me a million times that whatever goes on inside there has to be private. And who knew what Fancy Shoes might start suspecting?

I made a quick leap for the bottom stair and managed to be standing there, rubbing my eyes, when they came through the door. "Just getting up, Tommy?" Dad asked. "Or were you up there in bed reading those silly stories about Tarzan and Robin Hood?"

See what I mean about Dad?

"Tommy," he went on, "I'd like you to meet Mr. Avery Katkus."

Avery Katkus—so that was Fancy Shoes' real name.

He was almost as tall as Dad, but a lot fatter. Little wisps of hair were all that kept him from being completely bald, and his round face was all shiny with sweat.

He gave me a toothy smile and a handshake that was like gripping a warm sponge.

"Would you care for some coffee, Mr. Katkus?" Dad asked. "I think there's some brewing in the kitchen."

"Thank you, no," said Katkus. "My man Shandy's waiting outside, and he's probably getting impatient."

I glanced through the window. At the curb in front of the house, leaning against the fender of a long black car, was a man wearing the same black boots I'd seen yesterday.

Shandy.

Dad went outside with Katkus, leaving me with my head spinning. Katkus and Shandy, talking about searching for something in Parnell House, while Books and Harry and I hid under the tree and heard every word. Horace popping into view, first the head and afterward the body, and then Essie, all wet and dripping. And now Katkus's lie to Dad about wanting Parnell House for a home when I knew he was looking for something out there and he'd rip the house apart to find it. In less than a day I'd had enough of being scared and confused to last me all year. I wanted to get together with Books and Harry the

Blimp to see if the three of us could figure out what was going on.

But what I did right then was tiptoe into Dad's office while he was still outside. Maybe there was something . . .

There was. On Dad's desk was a single sheet of paper with some typing on it. The letters weren't clear, and the typewriter must have been an old one. Still, there wasn't any doubt about the meaning of the words.

> To tHe Village Council of Bramton:
> I, Avery Katkus, submit tHis bid for tHe PAR-
> NELL HOUSE and grounds, witH full payment
> to be made at date of purchase.
>
> $40,000

Even with those capital H's after every t, that paper looked mighty official to me. Good-bye playground. Good-bye Horace and Essie. After gobbling down a bowl of cereal in the kitchen, I went off in search of Harry the Blimp and Books.

An hour later, the three of us were huddled together in the little shed behind Harry the Blimp's house. I started talking about Fancy Shoes being in Dad's office and offering to buy Parnell house while Black Boots waited outside, and how their real names were Katkus and Shandy. Then I made a big mistake. I told them about last night.

I'd no sooner got to the part where Horace put his

head onto his shoulders when Books let out a whoop you could hear a mile.

"Ghosts!" she shouted with a silly giggle. "Ghosts? Come on, Tommy. You've dreamed up a lot of things, but this one takes first prize."

"You're just funning us, huh, Tommy?" added Harry the Blimp. "You know ghosts ain't real. Just somethin' you imagined."

"They were right in the room with me, I tell you." I never expected my two best friends not to believe me. After all, what are best friends for?

"If I saw any ghosts," Harry went on, "I'd throw 'em down and sit on 'em. I wouldn't be scared like you were, Tommy." And he gave a loud laugh that made me madder than ever.

"What I think, Tommy," said Books, "is that you fell asleep in there and dreamed the whole thing. Dreams can be pretty real sometimes. And I've even seen you dreaming when you were awake. So let's forget about the ghosts and concentrate on Katkus and Shandy."

"Right, Books," said Harry. "You tell us what we should do."

I was pretty sore at those two. But arguing wasn't going to do any good. So I did the smart thing and kept my mouth shut.

"Okay," said Books. "First, I think we ought to try

and figure out what in heck those two are searching for."

"Maybe pirate gold," I suggested.

"Tommy, there's no ocean within hundreds of miles of here," Books scoffed. "Be practical."

She sounded just like Dad.

"How much did you say Katkus had offered for the house?" Books asked me suddenly.

"Forty thousand dollars. Why?"

"Then whatever he and Shandy are looking for has got to be worth more than that. A lot more."

"Then what—" Harry began.

Books just shrugged. "I don't know. And the only way we can find out is to go back to Parnell House. Tonight. Then if Shandy finds anything, we'll see what it is."

"But what if he sees us?" I asked.

"Then we run away—quick!"

"And the ghosts?" I went on. "What if we see—"

"I've heard enough about your stupid ghosts," Books sneered. "All those who think Tommy Donahue's imagination has got the best of him, raise your hand."

I was outvoted, two to one. No more talk about ghosts.

That night I waited for Dad to start snoring and then sneaked out just as easily as before. I ran all the way to Parnell House, but when I reached the gate I pulled up suddenly and crouched down low.

A shadowy figure was standing just inside the gate. In the darkness it seemed huge. Shandy?

"Tommy, is that you?"

The breath rushed out of me like an engine letting off steam. It was Harry the Blimp.

"I forgot a flashlight," he said. "I had to wait in the dark."

"Don't worry about it. I brought a big candle with me. Where's Books?"

"Right here" came a voice from up the block. I turned about and saw Books coming toward us on the sidewalk.

We groped our way around to the back door. I waited until we were inside before lighting the candle. No sense letting everybody in town know we were there.

Books put her lips close to my ear. "Where's the room you hid in yesterday night, Tommy," she breathed. "I want to meet those ghosts of yours."

"They—they don't always show themselves," I whispered back. "Maybe they won't—"

"Sure, Tommy. Sure. Just show me the room."

We creaked our way upstairs and went into the bedroom where I'd seen Horace and Essie. Only now it was deserted.

"Hello there, Parnells," called Books softly. "Come out, come out, wherever you are."

"Cut it out, Books," I hissed. "They have to decide whether they like you before—"

"Here, ghostie, ghostie, ghostie. Come to Books."

"Shut up, you two," ordered Harry the Blimp suddenly. "And blow out that candle. Listen!"

I put out the candle, and the three of us stood shivering in the darkness. Then we all heard it.

The crunch, crunch of heavy feet walking through the dead weeds outside the house. Steps on the rotting floor below. Finally, the creak of somebody coming upstairs.

"The closet," Books said in a frightened whisper. "It's the only place to hide."

Before I had time to think what might jump out at us, Books had the closet door open, and Harry the Blimp was dragging me inside. Books closed the door until only a small crack remained. We peered through the crack.

Suddenly a man entered the bedroom holding a hissing gas lantern that made a light so bright it hurt my eyes. In the man's other hand was a big, curved crowbar.

It was Shandy.

He set the lantern down on the small table where Horace's head had appeared. Then he rubbed his hands together like a workman getting ready to do his job.

"By morning I'll have this room torn apart," he muttered with a harsh laugh. "If there's anything hidden here, I'll find it for sure."

Horace vs. Shandy

While Books and Harry the Blimp and I squinted through the crack in the closet door, Shandy raised the crowbar and brought the straight end down between two floorboards with a loud *thunk*.

Rusty nails screeched as he pried the board up. He tossed it aside and looked into the opening. "Nothing," he muttered. He raised the crowbar again.

Do you remember earlier how I told you I could be depended on to do the wrong thing, whatever was going on? Well, right there in the closet, I did it again.

I started to sneeze.

I could feel it coming, and I tried to hold it in. I pinched my nose with one hand and put the other one over my mouth. But the sneeze got stronger and stronger. It was going to come out, no matter what. I held on as long as I could until finally . . .

"*Aaaahh . . . choooo!*"

Shandy jerked back like somebody'd kicked him. Then he turned and stared long and hard at the closet. He was holding the crowbar near the bottom, like a club. He took a step toward the closet.

We couldn't stand it any longer. With loud yells, we threw open the door, and Harry the Blimp and Books and I tumbled out into the room.

For a second, Shandy just stared at the three of us as if we'd dropped down from the moon or something. I think if we'd made a dash for the door right then he'd have been too surprised to stop us. But then Books had to go and open her mouth.

"Don't make a move!" she shouted. "We've got you dead to rights, Shandy."

Saying that wasn't the smartest thing Books ever did. I mean, Shandy was even bigger'n Harry the Blimp, and he had that crowbar, besides. He scowled at us and raised the crowbar over his head.

We jerked backward just as Shandy swung the crowbar. The curved end of it whooshed through the air only inches from my face. He moved closer and raised the bar again. We were goners, for sure.

"You're at your best when scaring young'uns, aren't you, Mr. Shandy!" came a stern voice from the far end of the room. "D'ye have the stomach to stand up to me?"

Shandy snarled angrily and whirled about. But when he saw the thing standing next to the little table, he froze in place like he'd been turned to stone.

It was Horace. And he seemed as real and solid as any human.

But no human ever held his head underneath his arm, the way Horace did.

Books and Harry the Blimp took one look at Horace and shrank down into a corner, shivering all over and whimpering like babies.

"Horace!" I cried. "Am I ever glad to see you."

"Move aside, young Thomas," said the head grimly. "For I'd not see you harmed while I deal with yon scoundrel."

Horace set his head firmly onto his shoulders and then beckoned with one hand. "Come, Mr. Shandy, if ye've the backbone for it. Come, do battle with me."

Shandy was quivering all over, and his face was slick with sweat. But he was ready to fight. In two long bounds he sprang across the room, swinging the crowbar like a club. If Horace had been human, it would have shattered his ribs.

But instead, the crowbar went *through* Horace and thudded against the wall. Shandy couldn't believe his eyes. They were telling him something his mind just couldn't accept.

"You missed me," sneered Horace.

"I—I didn't miss," Shandy gasped. "I hit you—I mean—"

Without warning, he lurched forward, swinging a fist the size of a bowling ball. A real person would have been knocked flat. But on Horace the fist had about as much effect as hitting a moonbeam.

Shandy stood with his head lowered, gasping for breath. "Enough of this flapdoodle," said Horace. He reached inside his leather vest and pulled out the flintlock pistol he kept there. With practiced motions he took a powderhorn from a deep pocket, yanked the stopper with his teeth, and sprinkled gunpowder into the pistol's pan.

Shandy stared at the pistol as if it were a poisonous snake. "No," he whispered fearfully as Horace thumbed back the hammer. "You can't—" And his face went dead white.

Horace jerked the trigger, and I heard three sounds, almost as one. *Click*—the flint on the hammer struck sparks from the curved metal plate. *Whoosh*—the gunpowder in the pan flashed with a puff of smoke as the sparks dropped into it. *Bang*—the flash reached the powder inside the barrel, exploding it.

The roar of the flintlock was still ringing in my ears as I saw Shandy throw his arms wide. Then he slumped to the floor and lay still and limp.

"Horace!" I cried out. "You—you killed—"

"No, young Thomas," replied Horace with a smile. "Close as you may look, you'll find no blood on Mr. Shandy. And see—his breathing is deep and reg-

ular. He's but fainted from fright. You'd best bind his hands and feet before he gets his wits about him again."

There wasn't any rope about, and I had to make do with strips cut from Shandy's coat with his own knife. Finally I got him tied up.

Books and Harry the Blimp weren't much help. They just crouched in their corner, staring at Horace and babbling nonsense.

"Come here, you two," I said. "Come and meet Horace Parnell."

Harry the Blimp and Books approached Horace slowly. As I made the introductions, they tried to shake his hand, but with no more success than I'd had the night before. Maybe I should have felt sorry about their being scared, but the truth was, I was enjoying myself. I hadn't forgotten how they'd laughed when I'd mentioned ghosts that morning.

"Where's Essie?" I asked Horace.

"She's about somewhere," he replied. "But very timid about appearing with so many humans in the house. Truth to tell, young Thomas, I was exceeding reluctant to appear myself. But when that scalawag came at you with the bar, I grew furious. And I guess my anger overcame my dread of showing myself."

Horace stuck the pistol back in his belt and put a finger to his lips. "Not a word now, from any of you, about seeing me here, eh?"

"Not a word," I agreed. Harry the Blimp and Books nodded in awed silence.

"Then whatever story Mr. Shandy concocts, he'll be thought a madman," said Horace with a chuckle.

"But I still don't understand why the bullet didn't kill him," I said.

" 'Alive' and 'dead' are like two different places, Thomas. Imagine you and I being on opposite sides of a deep valley that's impossible to cross. We can see each other and even talk. But you can't reach out and touch me, and I can't touch you. That's why all Shandy's striking out and punching couldn't harm me, and why my pistol ball didn't wound him. Neither of us could reach across that wide valley that separates mortals from ghosts."

"But . . ."

"No time for shilly-shallying now. Mayhap some passerby has already heard the scuffling up here, or even seen the gaslight glimmering through a chink in the boards at the window. You three must leave. 'Twould not do to be discovered here."

"What about Shandy?" I asked.

"Inform the night watch, lad. They'll send a constable to fetch him."

"Huh?"

"I think he means we should call the police," said Books in a trembling voice.

"But give not your name, young Thomas. Our doings

must remain secret until we find what these men are after."

With that, Horace faded into nothingness.

We three got outside as fast as we could. As we ran across the weed-strewn front yard, Harry and Books kept close to me, as if I could protect them from things that might jump out of the darkness.

"I—I'm sorry, Tommy," said Books. "We really should have believed you when you told us about the ghosts." Harry nodded in agreement.

That made me feel pretty good.

At the pay phone on the corner, I called the police. They wanted to know my name, but I said I was just a concerned citizen reporting a man who'd been tearing up floorboards in Parnell House. We hid in the darkness until the police car pulled up and two officers with flashlights went inside. After we'd seen them half leading, half carrying Shandy to their car, we all went home. It was three o'clock when I crawled into bed.

And more than two hours after that when I finally fell asleep.

The next day, I didn't get up until after eleven. I was eating breakfast—or maybe lunch—when Mom sat down and looked at me real closely.

"Are you feeling all right, Tommy?" she asked.

"Sure, Mom. Why?"

"You've been sleeping so late the last couple of days. But you still look tired. There are dark circles under you eyes. Your father and I think you might be coming down with something."

Trust parents to start getting curious just when you don't need it. If Mom or Dad ever found out where I'd spent the past two nights, when they thought I was in bed, they'd have fits. And just the mention of Horace and Essie, and Dad would go into his patented two-hour lecture about how my imagination was driving him crazy, while Mom would rush for the phone to call the doctor.

I promised Mom I'd get more rest, and that seemed to make her feel better.

Harry the Blimp and Books were waiting at the shed when I got there. "Shandy's out of jail," Books told me, first thing.

"Did he escape?" I asked, feeling a little scared.

"Naw. The way my mother got the story, when they brought Shandy into court this morning, he was still shouting about how some guy with a head that came off had taken a shot at him. And the police never could explain how Shandy got himself tied up. The judge said everybody involved in the case sounded like they ought to be in an asylum, and he fined Shandy fifty dollars for trespassing, just so he wouldn't have to listen to any more wild stories. Shandy paid the fine, so he's free."

"Uh-oh. D'you think he'll come looking for us?"

"Not a chance. The judge told the police to put Shandy on the first bus out of town, and if he ever comes back, they should lock him up and throw away the key. Oh, Katkus was in court too, with a big sob story about how Shandy must have been insane to be prowling around Parnell House that way. Katkus swore up and down he'd given orders not to go near the place."

"Sounds like the old phony baloney to me," said Harry.

"Sure it is," said Books. "But if Katkus wants to look like a law-abiding citizen, buying Parnell House as a home for himself, he can't have anything to do with Shandy after last night."

"Law-abiding! Katkus is a crook, just like Shandy." And then a big smile spread across Harry the Blimp's face. "But at least we managed to get rid of one of those two bums."

"Before you're overcome with happiness, Harry," said Books, "just remember that Katkus is still after whatever's inside Parnell House. And with Shandy gone, he'll be sneakier than ever."

"But we won't let him have the house," said Harry. "Will we, Tommy?"

How was I supposed to answer that? I didn't know what else we could do to save the old place. But Books had an idea.

"Why don't we go and see Lester Dade?" she asked. "Maybe he'll know what's in the house that's so valuable."

I wondered why I hadn't thought of that myself. Lester Dade's the man who started the drive to get Parnell House made into a town museum. Over the years, Mr. Dade had gotten a lot of people interested in the idea. All they needed now was money.

If anybody had a clue about the mystery of Parnell House, Mr. Dade should be the man.

When we got to his house, Mr. Dade acted real glad to see us. "That old house has been a passion of mine since I was a boy," he told us. "Now how can I help you?"

We didn't dare start talking about ghosts. So Books made up a story about how we were getting a report ready for when school started. Mr. Dade ushered us into his library, polished his glasses, and put on a threadbare smoking jacket. Loose papers and boxes of books were spread about so we could hardly find the furniture, but Mr. Dade pushed some of the mess aside so we could sit down.

"Parnell House, eh?" he said, rubbing his hands together as if he was getting ready for some big job. "Let me see. Where should I begin? Why, at the beginning, of course."

He launched himself into the history of the old

house, starting with Abram Parnell and going on with the sons—including Horace.

Suddenly he scratched his head. "Horace Parnell," he muttered to himself. "You know, I heard that name quite recently. If only I could remember . . ."

That worried me. I wondered if Mr. Dade had seen the ghosts too.

"It doesn't come to me right now," he went on. "Oh well, to continue . . ."

It was nearly an hour later when he got to Essie's story. And we hadn't heard a thing that helped us at all.

"Esmeralda was a headstrong girl," Mr. Dade droned on. "The daughter of Morton and Therese Parnell. At the age of fifteen, she accompanied her parents on a trip south. One evening, on a Mississippi paddlewheel steamboat, she simply—disappeared."

"She fell over the side when she went to lean against a railing that wasn't there," I said. "She drowned."

Mr. Dade looked at me sharply. "How do you know that, Thomas? There's no record of how Esmeralda died."

"Why—uh—" I stammered. Books threw me a look that could have fried an egg. "Just a guess, Mr. Dade."

Mr. Dade waggled a finger at me. "Never guess about history. It's downright inaccurate." Then he got back to his story, and I breathed a sigh of relief.

"Esmeralda's parents were shocked and saddened by her disappearance, especially since the girl could never be buried in the family cemetery. They did everything they could to keep her memory alive. First there was the monument."

"The one in the graveyard?" asked Harry the Blimp. "The one shaped like a T?"

"That's the one. As long as Morton Parnell inhabited the house, he had burning torches placed in the sockets of the monument twice a year. For a whole day in July and another in the middle of October. All in memory of his lost daughter."

"But why'd he choose July and October?" I asked.

"Hmm. Well, July was when Esmeralda Parnell disappeared. Of course Morton would honor his daughter then. But October? It couldn't have been Esmeralda's birthday. That was in February. You know, Thomas, I'm just not sure."

I sat deep in thought. Still another mystery about Parnell House.

"And the mantel on the fireplace?" Books asked. "Did Morton Parnell have that replaced, too?"

"Ah, I see you've been doing a little research of your own," said Mr. Dade with a smile. That was the first time I'd ever heard sneaking around a spooky old house called research. "Yes, Morton had a new mantel fashioned from a single slab of oak. The inscription was carved by the finest artisan he could hire. 'Tho' you rest afar, you are in our hearts.' What beautiful words in memory of his lost daughter."

While Books and Harry were listening to Mr. Dade, a thought was prowling around somewhere in the back of my mind. But it was dim and unclear, like seeing a person through thick, heavy fog.

Another forty-five minutes or so, and Mr. Dade had finally brought us up to date on Parnell House. It seemed the Village of Bramton owned it now, having taken it over when the taxes weren't paid.

But although we questioned him several times, Mr. Dade couldn't think of anything valuable that might be hidden inside the old house.

"I still wish I could remember where I heard the name of Horace Parnell—or perhaps I read it somewhere," said Mr. Dade as he showed us to the door. "It was quite recently—some time in the past two weeks. I'm sure of that."

As we left, he promised to get in touch with us if his memory improved.

That evening I took Mom's advice and went to bed right after supper. But I knew I'd never get to sleep, what with all that had been going on.

The next thing I remember, it was nine-thirty Thursday morning.

Katkus Strikes Again

"Thursday," Books was saying. "The Village Council is meeting tomorrow evening, and they'll be voting on whether to sell Parnell House to Katkus. We're running out of time."

The three of us were in Harry the Blimp's shed. And we were all really worried. As the hours passed, Parnell House seemed to be slipping away from us forever.

"I wish I knew what the *thing* is that Katkus is looking for," said Harry the Blimp. "It'd sure make it easier to plan some way of stopping him."

When I heard that, the same feeling came over me that I'd had at Mr. Dade's house yesterday. It was like I knew something—something that would help. But I just couldn't remember it. I was pretty sure, though, it was connected with what Horace—or was it Essie?— had said the first night I met them.

The feeling was a little like playing hide-and-seek and seeing a movement out of the corner of your eye. But when you turn to look head on, it's not there anymore. The harder I tried to remember, the less likely it seemed I'd ever think of it.

"Maybe we'll get lucky and the council will turn Katkus down," said Harry the Blimp.

"Fat chance," I answered. "I bet a man as sneaky as Katkus can make things happen just the way he wants 'em to."

"Tommy, couldn't you get your father to—"

"What would I tell him? That I've seen a ghost? He'd just give me another lecture on how my imagination's always getting me in trouble. Maybe he'd throw out all my adventure books, the way he always says he's going to. If we're going to do any planning, at least talk sense."

"Maybe Harry's making more sense than you know," said Books.

"If you think my father's going to—"

"Not about that. I mean about the Village Council."

"Come on, Books. D'you think the five of 'em are going to listen to us? They'd say we're just a bunch of crazy kids."

"But maybe we wouldn't have to talk to all five, Tommy."

"Huh?"

"Sure, the council has five members. But what if

some of them already want to keep Katkus from buying Parnell House? You did say your father thought Katkus's offer was kind of low. Maybe a member of the council thinks so too. Or maybe at least one of 'em agrees with Mr. Dade that the place should be made into a museum."

"Well . . ."

"Tommy, if a couple of those council members are already on our side, that'd mean we only have to change one vote."

"If, if, if!" I complained. "How are you going to find out how they're voting until the meeting starts?"

"Mayor Peace ought to have a pretty good idea," said Books. "Let's go see him."

"Mayor Peace won't talk to us."

"I bet he will," said Books. "There's an election in November, and Alonzo Peace has to be cheerful and pleasant to everybody until that's over. It's part of the rules of being a mayor. At least that's what my father says."

I didn't like the idea at all. What chance did we have of getting in to see the mayor?

But Books was right, as usual. When we got to the village building, Mayor Peace said he could give us fifteen minutes.

The walls of his office were of dark wood, with framed pictures of Washington and Lincoln hanging on them. The mayor himself sat behind a desk big enough for five men. "Now then, children," he said when we were seated, "what can I do for you?"

First, you can stop calling us children, I thought. But Books remained cool and calm.

"There'll be a vote on Parnell House at the council meeting tomorrow night," she said. "We'd like to know if you think they'll vote to sell the house to Avery Katkus."

The mayor looked at me sharply. "Mr. Katkus's offer hasn't been made public yet," he said. "You must learn to keep your nose out of your father's business, Tommy."

"Last year," Books replied sweetly, "our teacher told us it's our duty to learn what our elected officials are doing. Now about the vote . . ."

"Y—yes. But some matters—like this one—must remain confidential. Especially to chil—that is, those not old enough to vote."

"My parents vote," said Books. "Just like Tommy's and Harry's do. They've got a lot of friends who vote, too."

"I—I see." The mayor closed his eyes and thought about this. "Quite so, quite so. The fact is, however, that all discussions about selling Parnell House have taken place in closed sessions, and we've allowed no word of our deliberations to leak out."

"Isn't that kind of unfair?" asked Books. "To the people who pay taxes, I mean?"

"Wendy, the community is split on this issue. Think of the hard feelings if it were to be made public. Oh, one or two of the council members wanted to tell the newspapers about our meetings. I made sure *that* idea was voted down. And all council members must abide by that vote of silence."

Books and Harry the Blimp and I looked at one another, and I bet we were all thinking the same thing. Mayor Peace was almost as sneaky as Katkus himself.

"What do *you* think, Mayor?" Books went on. "Do you think Parnell House should be sold?"

"Of course I have no final say in the matter unless there's a tie when the council itself votes. In that case, I can vote to break the tie. But personally I think we're very lucky Mr. Katkus made an offer for that ramshackle old house. He's very generous, is Mr. Katkus—very generous indeed."

"Mayor Peace," said Books, "was Katkus generous enough to give you money to make sure Parnell House got sold to him?"

At that, the mayor's face got all red and puffy. "Why . . . why of course he didn't," he sputtered. "I would never . . . my respected office . . . how dare you even suggest such a thing?"

Now Books knew Mayor Peace better than to hint that he might take a bribe. Sometimes the mayor could be a windbag, but he was honest. I suspected Books was just trying to get him angry. She was doing a real good job of it, too.

"Taking money that way would be against the law, wouldn't it?" she went on primly. "And if the newspapers should hear . . ."

"It's just not true!" the mayor howled. "And if you breathe a word of this outside my office, Wendy Scofield, I'll . . . I'll . . ."

Mayor Peace looked like he was about to explode. He stammered and ranted and bounced about in his chair like he was sitting on a nest of hornets.

"Mayor Peace, will the council vote to sell Parnell House or not?"

I guess that's when the mayor's anger really got the best of him. Books's questions must have nettled him until he couldn't stand it any longer.

"It's all the fault of that idiot, Claude Beecham!" Mayor Peace bawled suddenly. "Nobody can predict how he'll vote. If that stupid Englishman stops the sale of Parnell House, I'll—I'll—"

Harry and I just stared at the mayor in astonishment. But Books grabbed a pencil and paper from the desk and started writing real fast. Then she got up and motioned for us all to leave.

Mayor Peace was still howling like a cat with its tail caught in a door when we sneaked out of the office.

"Wow, Books," I said when we were all outside. "You're really something, taking on Mayor Peace that way, while Harry and I sat there like two lumps on a log."

Books's smile beamed like the morning sun. "Yeah, I was pretty good, wasn't I? And from what the mayor said, I'd guess Claude Beecham's vote is going to be the important one at that meeting tomorrow night."

"Then we'd better see him right off and talk him into voting our way," said Harry.

"Right," said Books. "But I'll bet Katkus knows about Mr. Beecham, too. If Katkus gets to him first . . ."

Then it was my turn to smile. "I've heard Dad talk about Mr. Beecham," I said. "Dad says he's the most honest man in the world. He acts kind of odd sometimes, but whatever he believes in, that's how he'll vote. Katkus won't be able to buy him."

We agreed to meet at the Beecham house right after lunch. When I got home, Mom said I'd had a phone call from Mr. Dade. I was to call back.

Mr. Dade sounded excited when he answered. "Tommy? Do you remember my saying yesterday that I recalled Horace Parnell's name coming up somewhere just a short time ago?"

"Yes, sir." I held my breath, wondering if Mr. Dade had found out about the ghosts.

"I just remembered where it was. A few weeks ago, I was talking with a friend who lives in New York City. He's interested in our local history, too. He'd just been to an antique auction on Park Avenue. He wanted to tell me all about it."

"But Mr. Dade, I don't understand . . ."

"One of the items at the auction was a collection of journals—that is diaries—of a Revolutionary War soldier."

"Uh-huh."

"Thomas, that soldier's name was Horace Parnell."

I could feel myself breathing faster. "Did—did your friend buy the journals, Mr. Dade?"

"Oh my, no. He bid, of course, but he didn't have enough money. The journals sold for nearly ten thousand dollars. Such things are very rare and much in demand. They were bought by Waverly Associates of New York."

"Horace's journals were bought by a company?"

"No. Waverly Associates were simply agents for the real bidder."

"And who—"

"Some gentleman named—oh, what was it? Avery—uh—Cattail . . . Catcall . . . something like that."

Avery Katkus!

"Th—thank you, Mr. Dade." I hung up the phone and just stood there like I was carved out of rock. Horace's journals. Katkus had read them and found out—what?

Lunch was tuna fish sandwiches, but it might as well have been sawdust for all I cared. Afterward I met Books and Harry the Blimp in front of Claude Beecham's house and told them what I'd learned.

"So Katkus knows something about Horace, huh?" said Harry the Blimp with a shrug. "That doesn't help a whole lot, Tommy."

But it did. That shadowy thing in my mind was getting clearer now. If only I could—

"C'mon, Tommy," said Books. "Let's go see Mr. Beecham."

When we knocked, the door was opened by a tiny, gray-haired woman in a gingham apron. Her face was all drawn and sad, and I wondered if she was going to burst out crying.

"Mrs. Beecham?" I asked.

"Yes, what is it?"

"We've come to see—"

"Oh, dear. I'm forgetting my manners." Mrs. Beecham forced a smile and opened the door wide for us to enter. "Come in, come in, the three of you. I was just about to have tea. Perhaps you'd join me."

"We'd be glad to, ma'am," said Books. "And then maybe we could see—"

"In a bit, in a bit," chirped Mrs. Beecham. "First, our tea." She led us into the living room.

A big British flag was tacked to one wall, and on a table was a statue of St. George killing a dragon. A bust of Shakespeare looked down from the mantel next to a picture of Queen Elizabeth II, and the walls were covered with paintings of English country scenes.

"Afternoon tea is one of our most delightful English customs," said Mrs. Beecham, bringing in a steaming pot. "Both Claude and I were born in England, you know. We became citizens of this country nearly twenty years ago after Claude's work brought him here. But there's still a bit of England in our hearts. Have a biscuit."

She passed me a plate of little crackers. Then she poured the tea. With a cracker in one hand and a cup of tea in the other, I had a hard time balancing it all. Harry the Blimp put his cup on the floor until he'd finished his cracker. But Books managed everything like she'd been taking afternoon tea all her life.

"Now then," said Mrs. Beecham. "What can I do for you?"

"We were wondering if your husband is going to vote to save Parnell House or sell it," said Books.

"Oh, Claude had an awful time making up his mind," Mrs. Beecham replied. "Especially since his vote is so important."

"Just why is your husband's vote all that important?" asked Books, leaning forward eagerly.

"Why, I thought you knew. Two of the council members, Arabella Zale and James Bowmer, want to sell Parnell House. But two others—John Loring and Clarissa Gibbs—are against the idea. Mr. Loring thinks the price is too low, and Ms. Gibbs is on Mr. Dade's

museum committee. So you see, Claude has the deciding vote. It wasn't until this morning that he made up his mind which side he was on."

"And what did he decide?" asked Books excitedly. All three of us held our breaths, waiting for the answer.

"Claude would like the village to keep the house in spite of the money the village would lose," said Mrs. Beecham. "He said it would be a shame if the chance to turn it into a museum were lost. We English have a strong sense of history, you know."

I leaned back in the chair and glanced at Books. She grinned and winked at me. Harry the Blimp was so excited he bounced up and down in his chair. All our worrying had been for nothing. Katkus had failed. With Claude Beecham's vote plus the two others, the house would be—

"And Claude would have voted that way, too," Mrs. Beecham went on. "Except . . ."

Our excitement turned to icy silence. We gave one another worried looks and then turned to Mrs. Beecham.

"Except what?" Books asked.

"Except Claude can't be here for the voting."

"Can't be here!" squeaked Harry the Blimp. "Why not?"

"Well . . . Claude's mother still lives in England. In a little cottage near Crewe. And the poor woman suddenly became quite ill. She may not—I mean, perhaps she's going to—"

A single tear rolled down Mrs. Beecham's cheek. She reached into a pocket of her apron and brought out a sheet of yellow paper. It looked like one of those forms the telegraph company uses.

"This was delivered just a few hours ago," said Mrs. Beecham, handing the paper to me. "Naturally, Claude booked the first flight to England he could get. There was only a single seat available, so I was to come later. Oh, I do hope the British trains don't run late. Claude simply must see his mother again before—before—"

And she started weeping.

The telegram was typed on the form in dim, uneven letters. I read it once, and in spite of worrying about Parnell House, I felt sorry for Mr. Beecham and his sick mother.

Then I looked at it more closely. And suddenly I knew Mr. Beecham didn't have a thing to worry about.

But we did.

Claude,
Your motHer is quite ill. She may be at deatH's door. I believe tHe end is near. Come at once. Let notHing stand in your way.
                                    Pastor WitHerspoon

I'd seen those t's with the capital H's after them before. The same typewriter had been used to type out Katkus's offer for Parnell House—the offer I'd seen lying on Dad's desk. The message hadn't come from the telegraph company. It had been sent by Avery Katkus.

Mr. Beecham would arrive at his mother's cottage in England to find her in perfect health. By the time he returned, the Village Council meeting would be over. Without Claude Beecham's vote, there'd be a tie on the council.

And Mayor Peace would break the tie by voting to sell Parnell House.

Katkus! He'd tricked us again.

The Hiding Place

I'll bet you can guess where Books and Harry the Blimp and I went that night, as soon as we could sneak out of our houses.

This time, as we tiptoed through the rear door of Parnell House, I had my candle, Books was holding a kerosene lantern, and Harry the Blimp gripped a flashlight in each fist. Among us, we had enough light to hold a party.

But we didn't feel like it was a party. We had to tell Horace and Essie that we'd failed—that in less than twenty-four hours, Avery Katkus was going to be the owner of Parnell House.

We climbed the squeaky stairs and entered the room where I'd first seen those two ghosts. We stood there for a long time, just waiting for Horace and Essie to appear.

"Horace," I whispered finally, "come and show yourself."

There was a flicker in a corner of the room, and for a moment Horace was standing there. But I could see right through him like he was made of glass.

"It's okay, Horace," I said. "We're your friends, remember?"

This time Horace appeared in solid form—or at least as solid as a ghost gets. I was glad to see that his head was already sitting on his shoulders.

"Forgive me for being so timorous, young Thomas," he said. "You're friends, to be sure. But consorting with mortals still comes hard to me."

"When Shandy was here, you didn't have any trouble appearing."

"Aye, lad. My outrage at his attack on you overcame my fears."

"Boy, I'll bet if you got mad enough, you wouldn't care who was around when you showed yourself," said Books.

"I hope I never have to put your theory to the test, lass," Horace told her.

"Where's Essie?"

"She's about," said Horace. "Essie! Come forth, girl."

Slowly Essie appeared, staring timidly at Books and Harry the Blimp. Those two weren't doing any too well in the bravery department, either. Seeing Essie for the first time, they looked just as scared as she did. I made introductions all around.

Essie got her courage up and came forward to meet

her guests. "A real pleasure, Harry," she said with a little curtsey. "My, what a stout lad you are. An' so charmingly shy."

Harry got all red and wriggled like a puppy. "Pleased t' mee'choo, too."

"An' Wendy. I just know we're gonna—" Suddenly a look of amazement appeared on Essie's face, and she pointed a damp finger at Books. "You—you're a girl?"

"Sure I'm a girl," said Books in a quavery voice. "What did you expect?"

"Oh, my dear child, I'm sorry your family is so poor. It must be hard, having no money for pretty things."

"I'm not a child," said Books. Even with the scare of meeting Essie for the first time, Books seemed to be getting kind of angry. "And my family's not poor. Where'd you get that idea?"

"Why, your clothes. Those worn trousers, an' the shoes that look like a pair of bedraggled carpetbags. I mean, really!"

Books looked down at her old sneakers and then back at Essie. "These clothes are comfortable," she said in annoyance. "Not like that stuff you're wearing. How do you sit down in that big hoopskirt, anyway?"

"A lady of real breedin' doesn't sit much," replied Essie. "She stands tall and erect and— Oh Wendy, I do wish you wouldn't slouch that way."

"Y'know, you're beginning to sound like my mother," said Books. "I don't need you telling me how to—"

"Have done, both of you!" ordered Horace sternly. "Now, what news, young Thomas? Have ye found a way to save Parnell House?"

Sadly I shook my head. I told the two ghosts about the council meeting tomorrow and the mean trick Avery Katkus had played on Claude Beecham.

"That scoundrel!" cried Essie with an angry stomp of her foot. "If I had him here right now, I'd— I'd—"

"Horace," I said, "did you know that Avery Katkus bought your journals at an auction a few weeks ago? He paid a lot of money for them, too."

"I'm only surprised he valued them at all. Truth to tell, Thomas, I rather lost track of my earthly property after—well, you know."

"I thought they might have some hint as to what Katkus is looking for."

"My scribblings? 'Tis doubtful." He sighed deeply. "So here's the end of it, I'd say. Katkus will buy the house and start right in tearing it down to find that— that thing he's looking for. And Essie and I will be homeless. Forced to roam from place to place until the end of time, with no spot to call our own."

"Horace—Essie," I said. "I'm sorry we couldn't—"

"Nay, young Thomas, don't lay blame on yourself and these two fine friends of yours. You've done all you could, and no one could ask for more."

After a glance at Books, he looked over Harry the Blimp from top to toe. "By George Washington's cocked hat, you are a big 'un, young sir," Horace told Harry. "I wish you'd been at my side that October day up near Albany when that British lobsterback was coming at me with his sword raised to cut my head off. He'd have thought twice about attacking someone the size of you."

Harry the Blimp got all red in the face. He was used to getting razzed on account of his size. And Horace was telling him it was an advantage. For Horace to find some kind words when things were going so bad for him—well, *noble* was the best word I could think of.

And then the strangest thing happened.

Click.

It was like a switch had been turned on inside my head. For two days a tantalizing notion had been playing around the edges of my mind, without my being able to think about it clearly. It was lurking there when we'd talked to Mr. Dade at his house, and again in Harry the Blimp's shed that morning. Those times, however, it had been merely the hint of an idea.

But as I listened to Horace trying to put us at our ease, it leaped out, full-blown and clear as crystal.

"Thomas, what is it?" I was so wrapped up in my own thoughts that Essie's voice seemed to be a long distance away. "You're staring off into space and not paying attention to anybody."

"The—the *thing*," I mumbled. "I know—"

"Tommy!" cried Books excitedly. "You mean you know what Katkus is looking for?"

"No, but—"

"But what?" Books sounded disappointed.

"I know where it is."

"You know where, but you don't know what," sighed Books. "Tommy, don't start getting our hopes up again. I mean, you get things wrong so often that—"

"Silence, lass," ordered Horace. "I would hear what he has to say. Go on, young Thomas."

What Books said was true. I did have a habit of botching things up. I hoped that just this once, I'd do something right.

"Horace died in October," I began slowly, "and Essie in July, like Mr. Dade said."

Harry the Blimp shrugged. "So what, Tommy?"

"D'you remember Mr. Dade telling us about Morton Parnell, Essie's father?" I asked. "He burned two torches—two of 'em—on that monument outside. And he did it twice a year."

"Once in July," said Books, looking at me like she was seeing me for the first time.

"And once in October," added Harry the Blimp.

"I think Morton Parnell wanted to remember not just Essie, but Horace as well," I went on. "He wanted a memorial to both Parnells who hadn't been buried in the family cemetery."

"But there was the mantel, too," said Harry the Blimp. "And the words on it."

" 'Tho' you rest afar, you are in our hearts,' " I said. "But the word 'you' could mean Horace as well as Essie."

"Morton Parnell remembered me—his ancestor—as well as his lost daughter," said Horace. "It touches me deeply. But what has this to do with what Katkus is searching for?"

"I think Morton Parnell wanted a part of you, Horace—and you, too, Essie—to be forever on Parnell land."

"A part of us?" replied Essie. "But our bodies were never found."

"Then something belonging to you."

"My emerald ring?" asked Essie. "That's the only thing of mine that Mama and Papa kept."

"And what of me, young Thomas?" asked Horace. "I had nothing of value when I died."

"I think you did, Horace. Remember, Avery Katkus bought your journals and he must have read through them. I'll bet something you wrote there got him interested in this house. What did you own at the time of your death, Horace?"

"My rifle. A tin lockbox and the clothes on my back. Nothing there of great worth." Horace shook his head in confusion.

"Maybe whatever Katkus wants is out in the cemetery," said Books. "Buried under the monument."

I shook my head. "Things rust and rot when they're buried in the earth. It's got to be somewhere inside this house."

"The fireplace—" Books began.

"Underneath the mantel, I think," I told her. "Where nobody'd suspect there was anything but stone and mortar. That's where we ought to look."

"But can the mantel be removed, Thomas?" asked Horace. "It's anchored tight. It'll be a strong person who'll break it free."

"I'm strong," said Harry the Blimp proudly.

"You certainly are," Essie agreed.

We left the room and went down the rickety stairs as fast as we dared. Books and Harry the Blimp and I clumped loudly from step to step. Horace and Essie just kind of floated after us.

On the main floor, Harry looked around until he found a big hunk of wood that looked like a length of hand-hewn beam.

"What's that for?" I asked.

"You'll see."

The fireplace was made of huge stones, and the opening was as big as a cave. Now, though, it was filled with bricks from the collapsed chimney outside.

"Tommy," said Harry the Blimp, "you and Books

stand right here with the flashlights and lantern aimed at the end of the fireplace. I want all the light I can get."

Books and I listened in surprise as Harry barked his orders. Usually he was content to let us come up with the ideas. But I guess he figured here was something he could do better than either of us.

"What are you going to do, Harry?" I asked.

"Do you see how the end of the mantel sticks out beyond the fireplace? I'm going to hit the bottom of it, right there. Something ought to tear loose."

"I dunno, Harry. It's a bad angle, hitting straight up that way. You won't be able to get much power in your swing."

"Want to bet?" asked Harry the Blimp. And before I could answer, he gripped the beam at one end and jerked upward.

Wham. The beam hit the end of the mantel from below. The whole house seemed to shake, and mortar dust danced in the flashlight beams.

I looked at the mantel. It hadn't budged.

"Maybe we should—" I began.

Wham. I closed my eyes as the sound pounded in my ears.

When I opened them again, I saw that the end of the mantel had lifted nearly six inches.

"My stars!" Essie exclaimed. "Such strength, Harry. You're a wonder and nothin' less."

"You did it, Harry," I said. "Now we can just lift—"

I grabbed the big oak mantel and pushed up. But I might as well have been trying to hoist Plymouth Rock. The mantel didn't budge.

"Let me try," said Harry the Blimp. He bent his knees and got one shoulder under the board. Slowly he straightened his legs.

There was a loud screeching and the air filled with dust. Sweat dripped down Harry's face, and he groaned loudly. He straightened up slowly, and the hand-forged iron rods that anchored the mantel to the stones pulled free. I thought that if the kids at school who teased Harry about his size could see him now, they'd be amazed. I never knew one person could be so strong.

For a second Harry the Blimp brandished the mantel over his head, and then he tossed it into a corner. Books wiped the mortar dust from her face as best she could and brought the lights over to the fireplace.

The layer of mortar on which the mantel had rested seemed at first to be flat and even—except for the holes where the iron rods had pulled out. But then Books pointed.

"Look, Tommy."

Near one end was a small hollow. In it was a tiny covered box. The box was black, but when I rubbed away some of the thick layer of tarnish, I saw it was made of silver.

I took off the top. Inside was a gold ring with a green stone.

"My emerald ring!" exclaimed Essie. "I never expected to see it again after all these years."

"Do you think that's what Katkus is after?" asked Harry the Blimp.

"Nah," said Books. "Even as an antique it wouldn't sell for enough to make Katkus pay forty thousand dollars for this house."

I pointed the flashlight at the other end of the smooth shelf. Something was there. It was flat and smooth, but not quite the same color as the mortar itself. I rapped it with my knuckles and heard a hollow, metallic sound.

"It must be a box of some kind, set right into the mortar," I said. "This is just the top."

The metal rectangle was spotted with rust and dented in several places. "Odd," I heard Horace murmur. "Exceeding odd. Rub just there, young Thomas, if you please." He pointed to one corner of the tin.

I did as he ordered. The metal shone dully where my thumb scrubbed the dirt away. And then I saw the initials, crudely scraped into the metal with a nail or some other sharp tool.

"Horace Parnell," I breathed.

" 'Tis strange indeed," said Horace. "It's my lockbox, right enough—the one I carried throughout my term in the Continental Army. At my death the box, along with my journals, was sent back here. But I thought it had been disposed of, long since. I never saw it here in the house."

"That's not so strange," said Essie. "Don't forget, Horace, during the sunlight hours we've been confined to our hiding place deep in the cellar. And certainly the workmen my father hired would labor only in daytime. Candlelight does not make for good craftsmanship."

"I never knew Morton Parnell had saved the box," said Horace. "Even in your father's time of grief over his lost daughter, Essie, he remembered to honor an ancestor."

"D'you really think the box is what Katkus is after?" asked Books.

"It has to be," I said. "What's in there, Horace?"

"Odds and ends are all. A medal fashioned by a blacksmith which I received for gallantry in battle, tho' I scarce deserved it. Some letters from my father and mother. A few personal papers. Nothing of importance, I assure you. Open it and look, if you care to."

"We can't open it while it's buried in the mortar. And we'll need a hammer and chisel to break it loose."

Books looked at her watch. "It'll be morning soon," she said. "We've run out of time. Another hour and the whole town will be up and about."

"But Books, we can't just leave the box here. We've got to—"

"We're too late, Tommy. We did all we could. And it's not enough."

"So it comes down to this, does it?" said Horace mournfully. "Not only does Katkus buy the house, but we've uncovered the thing that makes it valuable to him. Now it's his for the taking."

"I'm sorry, Horace," I said sadly. "I did my best for you. We all did."

"Blast that man!" Horace cried with a shake of his fist. "I've never even seen him and he makes my blood run hot with fury. Would that I had him here—in Parnell House—for an hour or two. Mortal or no mortal, he'd learn the rage of a Parnell wronged."

"Horace is right," added Essie. "Nobody should possess the deviltry and meanness that are in that man's heart. Were he to come here, I'd give him a piece of my mind, I would!"

The idea was a wild one. But what did we have to lose? I led Harry the Blimp and Books to a corner, where we whispered together for a couple of minutes. Finally I walked back to where Horace and Essie were standing in front of the fireplace. I gave them a big smile to hide the doubts I had as to whether my plan would work at all.

"If you want to meet Avery Katkus," I said, "then maybe—just maybe—it can be arranged."

A Most
Irregular Meeting

Friday—Village Council meeting day. In only a few short hours they'd be voting on the fate of Parnell House. I had something in the way of a plan to try and stop Katkus from buying the place. I just hoped it would work.

The first step was to find out where in town Avery Katkus was staying. In a village the size of Bramton, it wasn't that hard. I rode my bike around the parking lot of the Bramton Hotel without seeing anything, and Books didn't have any luck at the Sleepy-Tyme Motel, either. But when the three of us met back at the shed, Harry the Blimp told us he'd seen a long black car at the Sheffield Inn, and it sure sounded like the one I'd described to him as being parked in front of my house the day Katkus visited my father.

"What's next, Tommy?" asked Books.

I unfolded a map of the village that I'd ripped out

of the back of the phone book. Spreading it out on the workbench, I pointed to the Sheffield Inn.

"Katkus is sure to come to the meeting tonight," I said. "And he'll probably plan on being there early." I began tracing his route with my finger.

"He'll have to go along Master's Avenue—then turn right onto Spring Street. Yep—he'll drive right by Parnell House on the way. Perfect."

"And I'm supposed to bring my beach ball, huh?" Books asked.

"Right. And I'll be wearing my white jacket. I want him to see me without any trouble."

"Don't I get to wear something special?" asked Harry the Blimp, sounding disappointed.

"No, you just be ready with that wooden club of yours. Do it right the first time because you won't get a second chance. And Harry?"

"Yeah?"

"Did you bring the catsup?"

"Sure. A whole bottle." He pulled a red bottle out of his pocket.

"Give it to Books."

There I was, snapping out orders with all the confidence in the world. But deep inside, I was really worried. A beach ball for Books, a white jacket for me, Harry's wooden club, and a bottle of catsup. Would that be enough to save Parnell House from Avery Katkus?

———

At eight o'clock that evening, I was crouched behind the fence of Parnell House, peering through the leaves of a big bush. The sun was a red smear in the west, and I couldn't help wondering how dark it had to be before the ghosts could—

Then I heard Books hoot like an owl. She was in the middle of Spring Street, holding the beach ball and trying to look like she'd just happened to choose that spot to play. But now she pointed up Spring Street.

I looked through the leaves. About three blocks up the street a car was approaching. In what little light remained, I could see it was long and black. As it drew closer, the out-of-state license plates were easy to spot.

Katkus was coming.

Books tossed the ball in the air and let it bounce on the pavement. Then she waved her arms about like she was really excited.

Come on, come on, I thought impatiently. If Katkus didn't see her there in the street, our whole plan would be ruined. To say nothing about what might happen to Books herself.

Finally there was the beep of a horn, and the car slowed down. Books stayed where she was. The car swerved to the right. Books crowded it nearer the curb.

Then a lot of things happened real fast. As the car

darted by her, Books pounded on the front fender with her fist, as hard as she could. Then she staggered across the street, tumbled to the ground, and lay still.

Well, almost still. But I knew she was shaking catsup from the bottle she'd hidden in the weeds. And she was smearing the catsup all over her face.

The car screeched to a halt. The driver opened the door and got out.

It was Katkus. I breathed a sigh of relief. He hadn't hired somebody else to drive him around and help with his dirty work.

While Katkus puffed his way across the street to where Books was lying, I crept through the front gate. As fast as I could, I scuttled toward his car. The right door was open, and the engine was running.

Katkus bent over Books. "I—I didn't mean to hit you," he said with a kind of whimper in his voice. "But you jumped right in front of me. Oh, please be all right. Please!"

The way Katkus carried on kind of surprised me. I mean, he sounded like he was really sorry for Books. And I'd never thought of Katkus as being sorry about anything.

But I had work to do. I reached inside the car, turned the key, and yanked it out of the ignition. Just then I heard a cry behind me.

"Catsup!" Katkus howled. "It's not blood. It's nothing but catsup! What are you trying to—"

Suddenly Books shoved on Katkus's shoulders, and he tumbled over backward. She jumped to her feet and ran off down the street. Katkus was just getting up when I called to him.

"Hey, Mister! I've got your car keys. If you want them back, you're going to have to catch me first." I held the key ring over my head and jingled the keys loudly.

"Hey, what are you doing? Why, you little—"

Katkus lurched toward me. But already I was running to Parnell House. I put the keys in my pocket and took out my flashlight. I didn't want Katkus getting too close. But I didn't want him to lose me, either.

Katkus was puffing behind me as I ran across the yard. Every couple of seconds I'd blink the flashlight so he wouldn't lose me in the dark. We raced around the house, and I plunged through the rear door and turned off the flashlight at the same time.

Parnell House was all dark. Crouched at the foot of the stairs, I could hear Katkus's heavy breathing as he came inside.

"Okay, son," he puffed. "Fun's fun, but I have an appointment to keep. So just give me the keys, and let's have no more trouble."

I didn't move a muscle.

"Where are you, you little monster?" he shouted out. "When I get my hands on you—"

Suddenly I snapped on the flashlight. At the same

time I started upstairs, taking the steps two at a time. "You can't catch me!" I yelled. As I reached the top, I heard a creaking down below, and I knew he was coming after me.

With the light still on, I ran into the room where I'd first met Horace and Essie. *Creak, creak, creak . . . clump.* Katkus had reached the second floor.

For a moment there wasn't a sound. Then Katkus tiptoed toward the room where I was hiding. "I see your light," he growled harshly. "You won't get away now."

I switched off the light and hid behind the door, just as he clumped heavily into the room. As soon as I heard his footsteps move to the center of the room, I dashed back out into the hall, slamming the door behind me. In the darkness it took a couple of seconds to locate the stairs, but then I started running down them. Halfway to the bottom I tripped and fell the rest of the way, banging one shoulder hard when it hit the floor. Upstairs, I could hear Katkus scratching at the door of the room and trying to find the knob.

"Now, Harry!" I screamed. "Now!"

Harry the Blimp came charging out of the dark corner downstairs where he had been hiding. In his hands was that same hunk of wood he'd used to break loose the mantel.

The stairs ran along the center wall, and two great posts supported them on the other side. Harry stepped

up to one of the posts and swung his club like a cave-
man killing a mammoth.

Crack.

The post, soft and rotten, flew out of its place and
fell to the floor. Before it had landed, Harry was
swinging at the other one.

Crack.

With the second post gone, the stairs had nothing
holding them up on that side. Slowly, and with much
creaking and groaning, they pulled away from the
wall. Then, with a loud crash, they fell to the floor,
not stairs anymore but just a big pile of wood.

"Now you've done it, boy!" I heard Katkus howl.
"When I get my hands on you, I'll make you sorry
you were ever born!"

I turned on the light and swung it upward. Through
the cloud of dust raised by the collapsing stairs, Harry
and I could see Katkus, standing there and shaking
his fist. But where the stairs used to be, there was
now—nothing. To get back down, Katkus would have
to jump—or fall—nearly twelve feet.

"Go find me a ladder!" Katkus ordered. "Get me
down from here at once!"

"We're fresh out of ladders," answered Harry. "So
I guess you'll have to stay up there. Unless you can
fly down like a bird."

For a second Katkus just stood there at the edge
of the second floor. He seemed to be judging the

distance he'd have to fall. Then he moved back a couple of steps and crouched down like he was getting ready for a running start.

"He's going to do it!" Harry cried, looking at me in alarm. "He's going to jump!"

"Oh, I wouldn't do that if I were you, Mr. Katkus," I heard a girl's voice say from up there. "If you try it, you're gonna break your neck."

And suddenly there was Essie, standing right in front of Katkus at the edge of the second floor. But she wasn't quite solid. All of us—including Katkus—could see right through her.

"*Aaayeeee!*" Katkus's scream of terror was inhuman, like that of a monkey, or a puppy in awful pain. And when Horace appeared beside Essie, holding his head in his hands, Katkus turned a pasty white, and strange gurglings came from his throat.

Slowly the ghosts advanced toward the horrified man. Just as slowly, he inched his way backward. Back—back—toward the door of the room. Katkus backed inside, holding out a hand as if to ward off the stalking ghosts. But they followed him inside.

Then Horace's head, clutched tightly in his hand, appeared around the edge of the door. "You three had best get to your meeting, young Thomas," said the head. "We'll entertain Mr. Katkus while you're gone."

Just as Harry and Books and I reached the door,

a scream rang in our ears. Then another. And another.

"Have a good evening, Mr. Katkus," I called into the darkness.

The meeting of the Bramton Village Council was well under way by the time we got there. Scarcely twenty-five people had turned out.

At a long table in the front of the room sat four members of the council. There was a fifth chair, but it was empty. I figured that's where Mr. Beecham would have been sitting if Katkus hadn't sent him on that wild goose chase to England.

Mayor Peace sat at a desk next to the table. Beside him was my father, with an armful of papers that he kept shoving in front of the mayor, a few at a time. Once in a while Dad would whisper in the mayor's ear, and then they'd both nod wisely.

When Dad spotted Books and Harry and me walking down the aisle and taking seats, he gave me a look that if it'd been daggers, it would have sliced me to ribbons. But of course he couldn't say anything right in the middle of the meeting.

Mayor Peace was going on about how he was saving the people all kinds of money. But when he finally got to the point, he had to announce that taxes were going up anyway. After a while, I began to think the vote on Parnell House wouldn't ever come up.

But finally it did.

"Ed Donahue, our village attorney, has presented me with an offer from Mr. Avery Katkus to buy Parnell House," said Peace pompously. "Forty thousand dollars. It seems to me most generous for that wreck of a house. I call for a vote on this."

"Wait a minute," said one of the onlookers. "Mr. Katkus doesn't seem to be present. Shouldn't he be here, since he's the one making the offer?"

Harry the Blimp and Books and I looked at one another with satisfied nods. How can somebody buy a house, we were thinking, if he isn't there when it's to be sold?

But it took Mayor Peace about ten seconds to wreck all our planning.

"I grant Mr. Katkus's absence is somewhat unusual," he said. "But the offer has been made in proper form. And therefore it must be voted on, one way or the other. All those council members in favor of accepting Mr. Katkus's offer, please raise your hands."

Arabella Zale and James Bowmer lifted their right arms.

"All opposed?"

John Loring and Clarissa Gibbs raised their hands.

Books and Harry and I were in shock. Our playground was being sold with no more ado than there'd be in selling a loaf of bread. Mayor Peace droned on.

"Claude Beecham, our fifth member, is away on urgent business," he said. "It is therefore my duty to cast the deciding vote. And I vote to . . ."

"Wait a minute!" I was on my feet, looking about in surprise. It hardly seemed possible that *I* was the one who had shouted out.

"Thomas Donahue?" said the mayor, frowning over the tops of his glasses. "Is that you?" Then he turned with a scowl and began whispering with Dad.

"Yes, sir," I gulped.

"Irregular—most irregular indeed," murmured the mayor to my father.

"Tommy," Dad said in his angriest voice, "go home right now. You have no business here."

"But I do, Dad. You can't just sell Parnell House. I mean—"

"You get home this instant, young man, or you'll be confined to your room for—for a year! I mean it."

There were a couple of titters from people in the audience, and Dad got all red in the face. But he still looked mad enough to strangle a moose. I tried to slip back down into my chair.

But then I felt Harry the Blimp's hand on my back, pushing me up again. "Don't give up now, Tommy," he whispered to me.

"If—if you sell Parnell House, Mayor Peace," I said, scared all the way down to my toes, "where will the ghosts go?"

"Ghosts!" The way Dad roared out the word, you could have heard it on the moon.

"Yes, sir. Horace and Essie Parnell. The house is their home, and they can't ever leave it, but they sleep in the cellar during the day, and Mr. Katkus is with them now, so—"

"You and your confounded daydreams and imagination!" snapped my father. "I knew they'd get you into trouble someday. Well, son or no son, I'm going to—"

Somebody giggled loudly in the front row. Then a chuckle from across the room. And before you knew it, the whole place was one big roar of laughter.

And the laughter was all because of me.

"Ghosts!" chortled Mayor Peace, wiping his eyes with a handkerchief.

And then the back door of the meeting room banged open. It got quiet real quick, and everybody turned around. Chief of Police Myron Borchard marched down the aisle, followed by his deputy, Officer Wilson.

They went to the front of the room, and Chief Borchard began whispering in Mayor Peace's ear. Suddenly both the mayor and Dad looked straight at me. But the mayor wasn't laughing anymore, and Dad didn't look angry. More like he was—puzzled.

"Come up here, Thomas—and bring your friends, too," said Mayor Peace, beckoning to us.

At the mayor's desk, Chief Borchard was still whispering. "It was Katkus, all right. We could hear him screaming all the way down the block. He must have been trapped up there when the stairs gave way."

"They why didn't you rescue him?" the mayor demanded.

"Like I told you, sir," Borchard sputtered, "he wasn't alone. There were these—these two—I dunno what they were, all flickering into view and then disappearing again. One was all wet and wearing a funny dress. And the other one had his head—I mean—"

"What do you think I should do, Chief Borchard?"

"You'd better go out there, Mayor Peace. Bring Ed Donahue, here, and the members of the council, too. Katkus keeps yelling that he wants to see you. He says he's got something to say before those—those things— do something awful to him."

"You—you could see right through them?" the mayor asked.

"Yep. Like they were painted on glass. But they move just like real people. Except for that man's head, of course."

Dad was staring at me again. But now his jaw had dropped so his mouth looked like a great big *O*.

"Ed, perhaps your son should come along," said Mayor Peace. "And his friends, as well."

Books and Harry and I got to ride back to Parnell House in the police car with the siren going full blast, and Chief Borchard and Wilson in the front seat. When we got there, Wilson rigged up a pair of spot-lights that lit up the outside of the house. Over across the street, people were coming out of their houses to see what was going on.

"Wilson," Chief Borchard said to his deputy, "I want you to go in there and set up more lights. We can't have the mayor and his council stumbling over things in the dark."

Inside the house, Katkus screamed loudly.

"Do—do I have to, Chief?" Wilson asked nervously.

"There's nothing to be scared about," I told Wilson.

"But the woman in the long wet— And the man with his head—"

"Oh, that's just Essie and Horace. They're friends of ours."

"Friends, huh?" said Wilson. "Then how about you three setting up the lights in there?"

"Sure," said Harry. "Why not?" and he picked up a heavy searchlight under each arm.

From the lights Harry was carrying, wires trailed back to the police car in the yard. Books and I followed Harry around to the back door. Just as we got there, a station wagon carrying Dad, Mayor Peace, and the four council members screeched to a halt out in front.

We went inside, and Harry set up one light while Books and I got the other one ready. "Okay, Officer

Wilson!" Harry called when we'd finished. "Turn 'em on!"

The lights turned the darkness inside Parnell House into day.

"*Aaayeeee!*"

There, at the edge of the second floor where the stairs had been, stood Avery Katkus. His face was a dead white, his eyes stared in terror, and his mouth gaped open like a toothy cave.

Beside Katkus stood Horace and Essie. We could see right through Essie to the hallway beyond. And Horace had his head tucked under one arm.

Just then I saw Chief Borchard peer fearfully around the edge of the back door. Then he stepped aside so Officer Wilson could come in first. Both of 'em looked up at the second floor, and sweat was popping out all over their faces.

"All those people out there," said Essie timidly. "And the two standing there beside Tommy seem to be soldiers of some kind, judging from the uniforms. Oh, it's all so frightening."

"A pox on the lot of 'em!" roared Horace. "I want only to see the mayor of this town and his council." His head glared down at Chief Borchard. "Can you manage that, sirrah?"

"Yes—yes, sir," the chief said in a whisper. "They're right outside."

"If they're not inside at once, I'll have your guts for garters! Begone!"

Chief Borchard darted out through the door. Horace's head winked at me. "This is rather fun, young Thomas," it said. "Who'd have believed humans would be more terrified of me than I am of them?"

A moment later, Mayor Peace and the council members—and my father—crowded their way inside. "Now then, young man," said Dad. "What's all this nonsense about gh—"

And that's when they all caught sight of Horace and Essie, standing up there on either side of Katkus. Horace pointed at the mayor and the council with one hand and held his head inches from Katkus's nose with the other.

"Say on, you blackguard!" Horace commanded Katkus. "Tell these fine folk what ye've already told me. If not, you obese knave, I'll hold my head to your belly and nibble all the way through to your backbone!"

"*Yawp!*" cried my father, looking upward and covering his eyes with both hands.

And that's when I got the feeling I wouldn't be hearing much more talk around our house about my overactive imagination.

The Secret of Parnell House

Avery Katkus, his knees shaking and his face a sickly gray, stared at the group of people looking up at him. He opened his mouth wide, but only a tiny whisper came out of it.

"Louder!" Horace's head shouted.

"I—I'm a buyer and seller of antiques," Katkus began. "When Horace Parnell's journals of his life in the colonial army came on the market, I wanted them just to sell for a profit. I never dreamed I'd find out— I mean—"

Katkus's feet did a little dance up there, trying to keep him away from Horace's head. He kept getting nearer and nearer to the edge of the second floor, where the stairs had collapsed.

"I read the journals," he went on, "and I learned about Horace Parnell's lockbox and what it contained. I was sure the box was still in this house. I—I had to have it at any cost. I knew I needed somebody strong to help, so I brought Shandy along. The two of us decided to—that is—"

Katkus sputtered on for several moments. Finally he pointed to himself with a trembling finger. "I'm not a criminal!" he squealed. "I haven't done anything wrong!"

"You led us to believe you wanted to restore Parnell House and live in it," rumbled Mayor Peace. "But instead you planned to tear it down to find the box. Hardly the act of an honest man, Mr. Katkus. And to think, you made me an unwitting partner in your scheme."

"Yeah, and what about Shandy's attacking us with the crowbar the other night?" cried Books. "He could have killed us."

"We didn't set out to hurt anybody. We just wanted the box."

"Will you get to the point, ye vile scut!" roared Horace's head. "What's in the box that's so valuable you'd go to all this trouble? Tell us!"

Horace thrust out his head. Its teeth clicked alarmingly. Katkus took a step backward.

But he'd run out of floor. When his foot came down, there was nothing beneath it. He toppled over like a great tree falling. For a moment he seemed to hang in the air, a fat, flying dinosaur. And then he crashed down among the wreckage of the stairs below.

He lay there as still as death, with arms and legs

outstretched. Somebody on the council screamed, and the rest mumbled and muttered to one another. Upstairs, Horace and Essie began disappearing and then flickering into sight again.

"Let me through," Dad ordered. He knelt down beside Katkus and examined him carefully. "He's all right," Dad said finally. "Just a bump on the head. But he'll be unconscious for a while."

There was much groaning from the council members. "Now we'll have to wait until he wakes up before we can find out what he wanted," said Arabella Zale.

"Why?" I asked. "Why not just crack the box out of the mantel there and look for ourselves?"

"Good idea," agreed Chief Borchard. "Wilson, get a hammer and chisel from the police car. Break the box free."

"Yes, sir." And a minute later, Wilson was banging away at the fireplace, chipping off big chunks of mortar.

Toward the end, he had to be really careful so as not to damage the box itself. But finally the mortar was knocked loose on all four sides. Wilson gripped the box and lifted. The box came free with a loud, metallic *pong*.

Wilson placed the box in Mayor Peace's arms. The mayor raised the tin lid with a screech of unoiled hinges. Books and Harry the Blimp and I moved closer.

Upstairs, Horace had set his head in its proper place

on his shoulders. "Could it be my money that Katkus was after?" he called down. "There's near a hundred dollars in there. I was in the army two years, and they paid me well."

Mayor Peace took a bit of paper from the box. On one side was a kind of seal, and at the top were the words "The United Colonies" and "Seven Dollars."

The mayor looked carefully at the bill. "Worthless," he said.

"Worthless?" cried Horace. "But—"

"I know something about old money," Mayor Peace went on. "These are Continental Dollars, and even back when they were printed, they had little value. Now they have none. Oh, you might be able to sell these for keepsakes, but they wouldn't bring enough to interest Katkus."

The mayor pawed through the box again while the council members pressed closer. "What's this?" he asked, holding up a brown, cracked bit of paper.

"A letter from my father. Took near six months for it to get to me, being passed from one traveler to another who were heading in my general direction."

"And this?"

"My 'listment paper. Signed with an *X* by Sergeant O'Shea there at the bottom."

Mayor Peace slipped the enlistment paper back into the box and withdrew a large roll of parchment. "And this?"

"Naught but a letter of appreciation from some gentlemen in Philadelphia. I hunted and fished to provide better food for them than was available from the inns and publick houses. They presented me with this, just as I wrote in my journal. You remember, young Thomas. I spoke of that the first night you were here. But the thing's a keepsake, nothing more."

The mayor unrolled the parchment carefully so it wouldn't crack. After a quick glance, he started rolling it up again.

But then he took a closer look. A gasp of surprise escaped from his lips. "Horace," he said in an awed whisper, "just when were you in Philadelphia?"

"Seventeen and seventy-six," Horace replied. " 'Twas boring duty. But the congressional gentlemen admired me to a man, as you can tell from reading that."

"What is it, Mayor Peace?" I asked. "What's on the paper?"

"Look, Tommy." He held the paper down so I could see. The writing was all curly and fancy, and a lot of the s's looked like f's. I started to read.

In grateful acknowledgement of the services of our friend
—HORACE PARNELL—
His skill as a woodsman brought us delicacies of fish and game which graced our tables and gladdened our hearts during the months of deliberations of this Continental Congress.

Below the graceful writing were about fifty signatures. I recognized some of them. *John Hancock.*
Th. Jefferſon. Benja. Franklin. And more—many
more.

Mayor Peace held the paper as delicately as a soap
bubble that might shatter at the slightest jar. "Unless
I'm mistaken," he said softly, "those are the names of
every man who, back in 1776, signed the Declaration
of Independence."

"Declaration?" said Horace from above. "Yes, I heard
some talk of that from Tom Jefferson and a few of
the others. Written to George III, telling him why the
colonies should be free. 'Twas readied some time in
July, as I recall. But the paper you hold, sir, is no
declaration. Just a letter of appreciation from some
friends of mine. Where's the worth of it?"

"The worth!" exclaimed my father. "Horace, those—
those friends of yours risked their property and their
very lives to place their names on the Declaration of
Independence and so defy the British king. They were
among the first heroes of our new nation. Their signatures—all on the same paper—must be worth . . .
Would you know, Mayor Peace?"

"That's more in Lester Dade's line," replied the
mayor, scratching his head. "But come to think of it,
Lester once told me of an auction in New York City.
Among the items were two books that had in 'em the
signatures of every man who'd signed the Declaration

of Independence. The winning bid, I believe, was a hundred and twenty thousand dollars."

A murmur of surprise went through the council.

"And that was ten years ago," the mayor continued. "Prices must have gone up since then."

"So if we sold Horace's letter," said Councilman Loring, "we'd have money enough to restore Parnell House, good as new."

"It'd be a shame to sell it, though," Books said to me. "After all, Tommy, we went through a lot to find it."

"But we've gotta have—" I began.

"A real shame," Books went on. Her voice seemed to be getting louder all the time. "That letter's something nobody else in the world has got. I'll bet if it was on display here—right here in Parnell House—people'd come from all over to have a look at it. That sure would make this village famous."

I looked at Mayor Peace. He was staring at Books and listening hard to what she had to say.

". . . And the people would need places to stay while they were here, and food to eat, and . . . and everything. Bramton might turn into a real city instead of just a village."

"But Books, we have to sell—" Just as I started in talking, the mayor waved a hand that hit me in the back and nearly knocked me over.

"Sell that precious piece of paper and have it leave

Bramton?" he rumbled loudly. "Not on your life!"

Then how are we going to get the money?" asked Mr. Loring.

"There'll be money aplenty, I'll see to that. When word of the letter and the signatures on it gets around, folks'll be standing in line to contribute to rebuilding Parnell House. And not just the citizens of Bramton, either. People all over the state—no, the whole *country*—will want to help us out with what we're doing here."

"Are you sure, Alonzo?" Mr. Loring didn't look any too sure himself.

"Of course I am. I didn't get to be mayor without knowing how people think and act. We're making some history of our own here. Real, living history. Just let me make a few telephone calls. We'll have fifty thousand dollars in a week and twice that much by the end of the month, with no end in sight. I guarantee it. We'll make Parnell House a wonder, and nothing less."

For a moment Horace had a hard time understanding what was going on. But then a big smile spread across his face. He hugged Essie to him. Above the murmurings of the mayor and his council, I heard Horace say:

"We have a home, my dear. We have a home."

Then he turned to the people below him. "You've been fools to fear us, good folk of Bramton," he said.

"Almost as great fools as Essie and I were to fear you. But now, in place of fear, we crave friendship."

At this, everybody began clapping wildly. "Let's have a big welcome for Horace and Essie!" shouted somebody.

Cheering rang throughout the house. Then, in the middle of the general hubbub, Essie looked down at Harry the Blimp and Books and me.

"I have something to tell these three," she announced. Everybody got quiet, wondering what was going on. I felt kind of foolish, standing there and looking up at Essie.

"Stout Harry," said Essie. "Wise Books. And especially you, with your pluck, Thomas. Know that you three will always be welcome here at Parnell House. For in our time of greatest trouble, it was you who offered us help. And there is no truer test of friendship than that. You are the real heroes of this night. Thomas . . . Books . . . Harry—God bless you."

With that, the mayor and his council—and even Dad—began cheering again. I looked at Harry and Books. Books was laughing and crying at the same time, and Harry had a big grin and a tear rolling down one cheek. I was smiling, but my eyes started to sting, and I knew I couldn't hold back much longer, either. This was the biggest thing that had ever happened to any of us.

I couldn't help thinking that after all the times I'd

made a fool of myself in school, with my parents and my friends, it looked like I'd finally gotten something right.

Mayor Peace proved to be as good as his word. Within two days, contributions began pouring in from historical societies, veterans' organizations, Scout troops, and every other kind of club you could think of. Even private citizens sent in dimes and quarters and dollars from as far away as California and New York. The money just kept coming and coming, and the mayor's staff had to cart envelopes full of money from the post office to the bank three and even four times a day.

Avery Katkus simply disappeared from Bramton, and that's just as well. We figured scaring him half to death was punishment enough. We just wanted to get rid of him. I understand, though, that word got around to other antique dealers about the trick he tried to pull. His business hasn't been so good lately.

Parnell House stands as it stood two hundred years ago, freshly painted and sturdy, with both chimneys straight and tall against the sky, and with new shingles on the roof. There's hand-cut glass in the windows and proper furniture in every room. Horace's letter, now called "The Parnell Parchment," is displayed under glass right above the fireplace mantel where we found it. And people come from far and near to hear Lester

Dade or one of his committee tell about how three kids—and a couple of ghosts—saved the letter from being stolen.

Of course, Parnell House is only open from nine in the morning until five in the afternoon, so regular visitors don't get to see the ghosts. Few of them believe the tales they hear of Essie and Horace.

But by vote of the Village Council, Books and Harry the Blimp and I can go inside whenever we want to, day or night. So if you were to visit Bramton and ask us real nice, we could wait until after dark and then walk down Spring Street to Parnell House. We'd go up to that room on the second floor and sit in the chairs that are in there now, and we'd wait, listening to the village clock tolling out the night hours.

And maybe . . . just maybe . . .